Lock Down Publications and Ca$h
Presents

I0666490

I'MMA DIE
BOUT MINE
5

For All Mine, I'll Lay Yours

By
Aryanna

Lock Down Publications
P.O. Box 944
Stockbridge, GA 30281
www.lockdownpublications.com

Like our page on Facebook: Lock Down Publications
www.facebook.com/lockdownpublications.ldp

Stay Connected with Us!

Text **LOCKDOWN** to 22828 to stay up-to-date with new releases, sneak peaks, contests and more…

Like our page on Facebook:
Lock Down Publications

Join Lock Down Publications/The New Era Reading Group

Visit our website:
www.lockdownpublications.com

Follow us on Instagram:
Lock Down Publications

Email Us: We want to hear from you!

Dedication

This book is dedicated to Jada Boo, Charlie (two middle fingers), and the graduating class of 2024!

Acknowledgements

First and foremost, I thank God first for helping me transform darkness into light. I couldn't do anything without you. I thank my fans for their love and support because it gets me through the moments of self-doubt. I wanna thank all of the real people in my life. There's a list of you, and it would take a few more books to include everyone, but you know who you are. I wanna thank those people that continue to inspire me in some way. I deal with a lot of bullshit, and I can't always talk about it, but if you know then you know. Crystal, I love you for always being there and making me laugh. Joy, what can I say except that you're a beautiful person through and through, plus you're a gangsta! Lol. Shout out to all my nurses who never get enough credit for being the brains behind the operation! I wanna thank Jessica (the rabbit), even though I don't get to see you because YOU left a lasting impression on me. Shout out to Mack, wherever you are, just continue to be great. Thank you to the two women who move as one unit and are the definition of black magic, black excellence, and strong Black women (L.L.). LASTLY, I wanna thank all those who hate because I appreciate you. I'll say more once I write my 'tell all' book, but for now, I'mma keep it cute. To all my Goonies, what's rockin?! Chain Gang! LDP FOREVER!!!

Chapter 1

(Tynesha)

I could feel David's blood spray across my face as his body flew into mine and knocked me backwards. Shock immediately took ahold of me because I couldn't believe that David had gotten shot or that my bitch ass cousin, Shaomi, was the one who pulled the trigger. No words came from his mouth as he stared up into my face, not even a final insult for the pain and torment that I'd caused him within the last year. All he did was smile at me, and then his eyes closed as a sigh escaped from somewhere deep within him. That made my soul shiver.

"No, David, you can't go. Not like this. Not like this," I said softly, holding him tighter and rocking back and forth like I was trying to quiet the screaming in my head.

The complete chaos swirling around us seemed unreal until David's men tried to pull his body away from me.

"Don't touch him! Let him go!" I screamed, blinded by the tears pouring from my eyes.

"Ty, let them help," Carrie said, taking ahold of my shoulders.

"He's-He's my husband, and they can't take him," I insisted, still clutching him tighter than I had the first time we'd made love.

"Sweetheart, I know he's your husband, but you've gotta let him get helped. He's gonna die if you don't let him go," Carrie replied gently.

When her words finally penetrated the fog of my mind, I was able to realize that he was still breathing, and that allowed me to release him.

"I'm going with him," I declared, hopping to my feet and following the men carrying David to a nearby green Range Rover.

By the time they'd opened the door to maneuver him into the backseat, I'd already sprinted to the other side and hopped in so that I could pull him into my lap. I could hear the men struggling under his 6'2", two hundred sixty-five pounds, lifeless frame, but I felt like I had the strength of ten men as I helped pull him all the way into my lap.

"Go! Go! Somebody drive!" I yelled, tasting the panic that was coursing through my body.

A few seconds later, the engine roared to life, and we were speeding away from the compound, leaving dust in our wake. I had no idea how far the hospital was from our location, but I was steadily praying to any god that could hear me to save David's life. There may have been many times in the last year when I wished death on him, and I'd even fantasized about killing him myself, but now that the possibility of death was real, I wanted to take all of those moments back. Not just for me but for the kids that he never had a chance to meet.

"Just hang on, David. We're getting you to the hospital," I whispered, holding his head and stroking his hair lovingly.

One of the soldiers was in the backseat with us, keeping pressure on David's bullet wound to slow down the bleeding, but the smell of blood was still overpowering, and I had to fight not to gag. I tried not to think about it, but the reality of what was happening made a mental escape impossible. I didn't know what to do, and that was the one thought clouding my mind like rush hour traffic on a holiday.

"You-You can't die on me goddamnit! You're all I have left, and you owe our kids a chance to get to love the most amazing father that they could ever have. Do you hear me,

King David? You CAN'T die on me. I won't allow it," I said, keeping my lips close to his ear.

I studied his face, looking for any indication that he could hear me, but he didn't flinch in the slightest, and that only increased my fear.

"Drive faster," I demanded, feeling his life slip away with each passing second.

"We're almost there, my queen," replied the driver.

"Just hold on, David. Hold on, baby, please," I whispered, kissing his cheeks, lips, and eye lids.

If it had been at all possible, I would've breathed life back into him my damn self, but instead, all that I could do was hope God was hearing the prayers from my sinning soul. When we finally slid to a stop in front of the one-story hospital building a few minutes later, there were nurses and doctors standing outside, waiting.

"My queen, you must allow them to take the king," the soldier in the back with us stated.

I didn't argue or fight this time. I simply kissed my husband on the lips once more and nodded in acceptance. As quickly as they could, the soldiers pulled him from the truck, laying him on the waiting stretcher, and then they disappeared with him inside of the building. My brain was yelling at me to get out and follow them inside, but my body refused to comply with this mental directive. It was like I was just glued to the seat that I was in, and the physical presence of David was still there in my lap. Nothing made sense though. Not David getting shot, not Shaomi doing the shooting, and definitely not Shaomi trying to shoot me. I understood that there was no love between her and I, but her actions had been some on sight shit, no warning. My instincts told me that this had something to do with the accusations that David had made about me kidnapping his uncle, which I knew were absolutely untrue, but it meant there was some shit in the game. I had to let the nurses and doctors help David, but I could help him by figuring out what the fuck was really going on. A brief tap on the truck's window startled me out of my thoughts, but the recognition of Carrie's face curbed the adrenaline that had spiked in my veins. I opened the door and stepped out, hating the feeling of my shirt sticking to my chest as a result of me being covered in David's blood.

"Wh-What are you doing here?" I asked.

"I wasn't gonna leave you alone at the hospital at a time like this, so..."

"No, I mean what are you doing in Ghana, Carrie? And what the fuck is going on?" I asked.

"It's a long story."

"Make it short," I demanded, looking at her like she was an easy target for me to unload the rage I was feeling.

"Okay. The short version is that David called me for help to track down you and his son, Rashon, but we were always a few steps behind you. When we got to Mexico, we heard that you were there, and we were trying to figure out where you might be. Then you sent that video to David saying that you were coming to him for help..."

"I never sent David a video about anything," I objected quickly.

"Yes, you did, Ty."

I took a step closer to her, not giving a fuck about her few inches of height advantage because I knew that my heart was bigger and uglier.

"I said that I didn't send him any video, so what part are you not understanding?" I asked in a soft, deadly tone.

"Well, if you didn't send it then you must have one hell of a stunt double or..."

"A twin," I said, finishing her thought.

I was surprised that it had taken me this long to consider Tesha as an option to explain the unexplainable, but now it made too much sense.

"So, then, it was Tesha who sent that video... and it was Tesha who showed up at David's compound, kidnapping his uncle," Carrie said.

"But why though? What was her plan?"

"I don't know. It could've been as simple as misdirection. All I know is that she was definitely impersonating you, and she has everyone thinking that you came to Ghana with a team of African hittas to kill everyone moving. Including Shaomi," she replied.

Hearing this put part of the picture into focus, and now I understood why Shaomi had gone guns hot as soon as she'd seen me. I had no doubt that her reaction would've been the same no matter if it was me or Tesha that she'd seen, considering how she'd fucked us both over. Knowing this helped me to understand part of my twin's motivation for coming here because I would've bet my life that she wanted to kill our cousin as badly as I did.

"Okay, so, a video was sent, and that's what brought you and David back here?" I asked, thinking out loud.

"Like I said, she was trying to kill everyone. I told David that it didn't make sense that you would attack him like this and that there was no way you'd managed to build an army while you were on the run with a newborn."

"Well, thanks for the vote of confidence," I replied, taking a small step back so that we weren't standing toe to toe.

When I moved, I got a sudden feeling of lightheadedness, and I had to brace against the Range Rover for a second.

"Are you okay?" Carrie asked.

"Yeah, I'm-I'm fine. I just..."

A sharp pain in my left shoulder caught my attention and made me pull my shirt down away from my collarbone.

"Oh, shit, you got shot," Carrie said, sounding as shocked as I felt.

"I got-I got what?"

"Ty, that's a fucking bullet wound in your shoulder, bitch, and it's bleeding fast. Come on," she said, grabbing my hand and pulling me toward the hospital doors.

At first, my feet wouldn't move to follow her because the shit that she was saying wasn't making any type of sense. When the fuck did I get shot, and how the hell did I not know the whole time that I was worried about David dying in my arms?

"Ty, come on," Carrie demanded, pulling me forcefully.

My choices were to either follow her lead or end up face down in the parking lot, so I chose the lesser of two evils and let her lead me Inside. When I walked through the doors, I expected to find complete chaos, considering that the peoples' king had just been admitted, but everything was flowing calmly like it was a normal day.

"We've got a gunshot victim here!" Carrie announced.

"Another one? That makes three," a nurse said, coming from behind the desk of the nurses' station.

"Three?" I asked, pulling up abruptly.

"Yes. The king and his wife and now y..."

"SHE is the king's wife, not the other woman," Carrie said quickly.

"What other woman?" I asked.

As soon as Carrie looked back at me, I knew who they were talking about, and I immediately reached for my gun.

"I thought you killed Shaomi," I said.

"Apparently not but I did park two slugs in her chest," Carrie replied.

"Where is she?" I asked the nurse.

"I don't-I don't know, miss."

"I'm your queen, and you will address me as such. Now, where is she?" I asked again, raising my pistol and taking aim at her face.

"Ty, don't!" Carrie said, trying to push the gun away from my intended target.

"Touch me again and I'll shoot you first," I warned, locking eyes with Carrie so that she could see just how serious I was.

She wisely took a step back, which made the nurse flinch involuntarily.

"I'm not gonna ask again," I said, stepping right in front of the obviously frightened woman.

"She's-She's in surgery."

"Lead the way," I instructed.

The nurse gave a slight nod before she turned and led me down a long corridor that carried us to the back of the hospital.

"Ty, you need to get your shoulder sewed up," Carrie said from behind me.

I ignored her and continued to follow the nurse as she took a left and then came to a stop three doors down on the right side. She pointed to the door that was labeled OPERATING ROOM #2, and then, she took several steps back. I wasted no time pushing my way inside the room with my gun still outstretched in front of me, ignoring the looks of shock that I got from the doctor and the nurse who were working.

"Step away from her," I instructed.

"We cannot do that because her life hangs in the balance," the male doctor said.

"Don't worry about her balance because I'm here to tip the scales. Now step away from her," I demanded again.

"Ty, you don't wanna do this," Carrie advised, coming to stand beside me.

"There's nothing that I want to do more in the world at this moment. I can promise you that," I replied passionately, feeling hot tears leak from my eyes.

"She's pregnant," Carrie blurted out.

My head snapped to the right like I had been backhanded, but I was merely searching Carrie's face for any hint of deceit.

"Don't lie like that," I said.

"It is true. This woman is pregnant, and we're trying to save both her and her baby. Please let us work," the nurse pleaded.

My mind was spinning, and I didn't know if it was from the amount of blood I'd lost or the news that this nothing ass, sneaky, conniving bitch was pregnant by David yet again. All I could see was red and with it came unimaginable pain from the heart that I thought was shattered so long ago. My hand dropped to my side, which prompted the nurse and doctor to get back to work doing what they did best. I was too mentally fucked up in the moment to stop them because all I really wanted was to go back in time and fix all that was broken. I wanted to go back to that first week that David and I had spent together in his condo, blocking the world out and needing nothing more than each other. Everything had been so simple then, even though Roland had been hell bent on complicating my life. I'd still had David, and we'd still had a future, but now, I felt like too much had happened for us to ever go back and recapture what we'd lost. Even though the race wasn't over, there was something inside of me that now understood that Shaomi would stop at nothing to get what she wanted. I'd been so blinded by family loyalty that I'd played right into her fucking hands, and now, there was no more family. My mother was dead, my sister was conspiring against me, my husband was no longer a man that I knew, and the only winner in all of this was Shaomi. It didn't make sense.

"How?" I asked aloud.

"How what, sweetie?" Carrie replied.

"How does she get to have it all? My husband... The kids that should've been mine... Even the love and respect that should've been mine. How does this bitch get to have all of that while the rest of us suffer?" I asked, trying to wrap my mind around this reality that seemed like an alternate universe.

"I don't know, Ty, but I know that David still loves you, even if he can't admit it to you. He proved that the moment that he stepped in front of that bullet for you," Carrie replied.

I acknowledged the truth in what she said, and it offered a tiny spark of comfort, but that didn't outweigh the reality of Shaomi's persistence. She wouldn't stop until someone stopped her.

"Step away from her," I said, raising my gun again.

"Ty, what are you doing. You can't..."

"Yes, I can, Carrie. I can do what the fuck I wanna do because I'm David's queen, and nobody will take that from me. Nobody."

I didn't wait to hear Carrie's objections or the pleas from the medical staff. I just fired two shots into Shaomi's face and released her soul into hell.

Chapter 2

(Tesha) (Mexico)

"Juan-Carlos? Juan-Carlos," I whispered sweetly.

When his eyes popped opened and locked on mine a few inches away, it was easy to see his confusion, especially considering that I was another woman in his bedroom and his wife was only a foot away. He quickly looked to his right to make sure that she was still sleeping, and that was when his nightmare became an inescapable reality. His wife was indeed in the bed beside him, but the wide gash I'd put in her throat that stretched from ear to ear made it obvious that death had claimed her.

"She complained that she couldn't breathe, so I did the humane thing and helped her out. Shall I do the same for your kids in the next room?" I asked.

My question immediately brought his eyes back to mine, and the blind panic that I saw let me know that I had his undivided attention.

"What do you want?" he asked.

"I'm so glad that you asked, Juan, because what I want is for your bitch ass to explain why you left my husband in Mexico City to get kidnapped by the Zeta Cartel?"

"I didn't-I didn't do that. You have the wrong guy," he stammered insistently.

"Really? Well, then, let me apologize for coming into your home like this because I thought that you were the same

Juan-Carlos who worked for Carlito. So, you're telling me that Carlito is lying?"

This question was asked as I was screwing the black suppressor onto the barrel of my brand-new Glock .34 that I'd been waiting to test out.

"Carlito sent you?"

"No, Juan-Carlos, he didn't send me. He simply told me everything that I needed to know about you and the people that you love. My father-in-law is a very powerful and persuasive man, and it was in Carlito's best interest to cooperate. So, you see, Juan, there's no point in lying now," I replied, smiling down at him.

Somehow the fear in his eyes morphed, and terror was born. This caused a tingle inside me, which forced me to admit that I was getting some type of twisted pleasure from this man's fear.

"I-I told him that we were in enemy territory not controlled by our people and that he was gonna start a war if he started some shit. He wouldn't listen, and he had demanded to be taken there. What was I to do?"

"You were supposed to do what you were paid to do, pussy!" I growled in disgust and anger, pushing my gun into his left eye socket.

"Please, señora. I'm all that my kids have left."

"You're not loyal, so I'm thinking that they'll be better off without you. You might be able to save their lives if you can tell me the best way to attack the building that's controlled by the Zeta Cartel where my husband is," I said.

"There is no way to attack without losing your life or your freedom because the Zeta's hold is strong on this territory. They have police and politicians in their pockets, as well as control in the streets. You would be a fool to go up against them."

"Yeah, well, I guess that makes two of us because you were a fool to fuck with my family," I said, pulling the trigger.

The silencer made the gun sound like little more than a cough, and the kickback from the pistol was minimal, even though the slug had caused the entire pillow to be covered in brains. I took a step back to make sure that he didn't suddenly start breathing again, then I fired two more shots into his heart before I left the room as quietly as I'd come.

"You find out anything useful?" Angel asked when I walked back into the living room.

"Nah, just more bullshit. Are the kids still sleeping?"

"Soundly," she replied, giving me a questioning look.

I knew the decision about what to do next was mine, just based on her look, and I appreciated that from her in this moment.

"Let's go," I said, leading the way back outside to the waiting black Jeep Cherokee that was idling.

I climbed into the back, Angel got in the passenger seat, and Destiny pulled off without a word.

"Where are we going next?" Angel asked.

"I guess back to the motel so that we can strategize our next move," I replied.

"Nah, we're headed to the airport. Dad wants everyone back in Russia asap," Destiny said, glancing over at Angel.

"Did he summon Free too?" Angel asked.

"Yep, she's already en route from Royal's compound in Nigeria as we speak," Destiny replied.

"Why do I get the feeling that this is bad news?" I asked, not liking the sudden queasy feeling in the pit of my stomach.

Neither woman offered up a verbal reply to my statement, but they exchanged another look that did absolutely nothing to assuage the slow build of apprehension that had moved up to my chest. My immediate thought was that Royal was dead, and no one wanted to tell me, but that notion didn't hold water because his sisters were too calm. The only logical explanation that left me with was that some news had been obtained about Royal, which could've come in the form of a ransom demand. I had already made it clear that I would pay whatever and do whatever to get my husband back, and I knew that his family felt the same way. I still wasn't trying to leave and go to Russia though because we might find an opportunity here in Mexico to take advantage of.

"Why don't you two just drop me off at the motel, and then you can head back to Russia to link up with the rest of the family?" I suggested.

"That's not a good idea," Angel said, turning in her seat to face me.

"What's not a good idea is leaving this country with no one down here to physically fight for Royal. Don't get me wrong. Power and influence work wonders, but the added threat of immediately actionable violence is needed too. It's all that the cartels understand," I said.

"I hear you, Tesha, but Dad said to come home," Destiny replied gently.

"If it was either of your husbands, could you honestly tell me that this is one demand that you would follow? Or would you stay ten toes down and stand on bidness?" I asked.

They shared another look, one that I could interpret as both understanding and sympathy because both of them loved their significant others with the same intensity that I did their brother. There was nothing that I wouldn't do for Royal, including give my life.

"We'll take you to the motel, but only on one condition," Angel said.

"Okay, what's the condition?" I asked.

"You gotta stay inside until someone arrives to watch your back out here," she replied.

"Do you really think that we can trust any of the cartel connections that we have right now? I mean, they've gotta know that a war of epic proportions is coming," Destiny reasoned.

"You're right, and I wasn't thinking about utilizing the cartel because I definitely wouldn't put any of our lives in their hands. I say that we stick to what we know and just use hired guns," Angel suggested.

"I know some hittas in Honduras. I'll make a call," Destiny said.

"And I agree to wait until they get here," I stated.

Angel stared at me with a knowing look in her eyes until I held up my right hand like I was silently swearing. After a few more seconds of eye contact, she turned back around in her seat, and I was able to breathe around the lie I'd just told. It wasn't my intention to be deceptive, but it was definitely my intent to remain useful to my husband, and I couldn't do that cooped up in a dingy motel room that smelled like old sex. Money talked anywhere in the world, and right now, mine was speaking Spanish to any nigga or bitch who had the answers I was seeking.

It took us fifteen minutes to get back to the motel, and I spent the entire ride trying to calculate my next move. I doubted that Carlito had outlived his usefulness, and at the very least, he would be able to provide me with useful knowledge about the Zeta Cartel. Everyone had a weakness that was waiting to be exploited, and I refused to believe that the Zeta Cartel was somehow infallible.

"Destiny, make the call and find out how long it'll take them to get here. I'mma call Dad and then make sure the plane is ready," Angel said as we all got out of the Jeep.

I followed them inside and went straight to the bathroom. I made sure to turn the sink on full blast before I stepped over to the toilet and vomited as quietly as I could so that I wouldn't be overheard. The smell of bile was an improvement on the bathroom's pungent permanent aroma, but the way it raced up my throat felt like tiny razorblade cuts. Even though I could acknowledge the part of me that enjoyed killing Juan-Carlos, I hadn't learned to fully suppress the attack of conscience that I got after moments like these. Part of me, albeit a small part, yearned for the day when only David would get blood on his hands because it maintained the illusion of my innocence. I'd come a long way and collected a lot of demons since then. There were times that I wondered if I even had a soul left, despite my hesitation to kill those kids back at David's compound. I could feel the shadows inside of me getting darker, or maybe I just wasn't fighting as hard as I used to in order to keep them at bay. All I knew for sure was that there was too much going on to have a moral issue with killing right now, which meant that I needed to pull my shit together with some quickness.

After I made sure that my stomach had no more offerings for the toilet to bless, I flushed and then ran the cold water so that I could put some on my face. I didn't dare put any in my mouth because the last thing that I needed was to be severely fucked up by Mexican drinking water. Once my composure was restored, I took a deep, calming breath, and then, I nonchalantly walked back out into the motel room. I expected to find Destiny and Angel gathering their shit together, but instead, they were huddled together around the phone in Angel's hand.

"Dad, we'll call you back," Angel announced, locking eyes with me.

"Make sure that you do," he replied, followed by a resounding click.

I froze where I was, sensing that whatever had my father-in-law in a foul mood had something to do with me.

"If this is about me staying here then I'll call him back and explain the decision myself because..."

"It's not about that, T," Destiny said.

"Okay, so what's the issue? I know that wasn't his normal tone, and I can tell by you bitches' body language that something is way wrong. So, what's up?" I asked, trying to prepare myself emotionally for complete destruction.

"It's your sister... Ty," Angel replied hesitantly.

"What about her?" I asked, fighting the sudden nausea that I felt return.

"Apparently, she's mixed up in this way more than we thought because the message that was sent to Dad was that Tynesha had been given the list of demands. Only she never told us a damn thing," Angel said.

"Wait, are you trying to say that Ty is the reason that Royal was kidnapped and hasn't been freed?" I asked.

"At this point, we don't know for sure. All we know is that she's very much aware of Royal's situation, and she was tasked with delivering the demands that must be met to secure Royal's release," Destiny said.

"But she didn't... And now, Dad wants her head in a nonnegotiable type of way," Angel mumbled.

"I see," I replied, finally moving from my spot right outside of the bathroom door and sitting on the bed's lumpy mattress.

The words spoken by Angel signified the test that they had all told me that would one day come, and I'd already accepted Ty's death as the ultimate conclusion, but... Something inside me was different now. If I had to put a finger on it, then I would say that hearing Shaomi gloat about the wedge that she'd driven in between all of us had brought about a different perspective by which I saw Ty. We'd both made mistakes, but the malicious intent wasn't ours when it came to viewing each other as opps. There was no doubt in my mind that her and I would've still had to shake something because of my decision to fuck David, but that would not have destroyed our family or brought us to this point. Where we were right now was a direct result of Shaomi, and maybe if Ty saw it that way then there would be some hope of reconciliation.

"Where's Ty now?" I asked, looking back and forth between them.

"No one knows the answer to that question, which is part of the reason that Dad is insisting that you come home with us to Russia. He's thinking that you may consciously or unconsciously know where to find your twin," Angel replied.

"Just because we look alike don't mean that we think alike. Besides, I already took and told you that I'm not leaving Royal here alone," I said, stone faced.

"Yeah, that's exactly what we told him right before you came out of the bathroom," Destiny said.

"Glad that we understand each other... Now, where does that leave us?" I asked.

Both women looked at each other for the answer to that question, but neither of them seemed confident in an idea or were eager to speak at all.

"Well, there's been no reports of Ty leaving Mexico, so I say that we look for her right here," Destiny stated.

"Well played, sis," Angel said, nodding in agreement.

Even though I nodded in agreement, my only thought was that I definitely needed to see Ty before anyone else did, or reconciliation would come in the form of a séance.

Chapter 3

(Royal) (Mexico City - Three Days Later)

Due to the fact that I was being held in a room that was blacked out, I'd lost all concept of time, in addition to the constant beatings that had become routine. Even without knowing the time of day or night, I was still able to recognize that a schedule had been set based on whatever Marta, aka The Red Devil, desired. Torture was on the menu for breakfast, lunch, and dinner, but Marta had made sure that the scheduled activities had different levels to them. The ass whoopings were standard procedure, but they were becoming more painful because my body wasn't given time to heal. By my count, I had at least three broken ribs to accompany the fractured orbital bones around my left eye socket and the two broken fingers on my right hand. The next level of torture consisted of starvation and dehydration because only when I felt like I was knocking at death's door was I given any type of nourishment or sustenance. The heat had been intentionally jacked up inside the room I was being held in, which only served to multiple the already humid conditions of the Mexican weather outside. The final layer of Marta's torture came in the form of the mental and emotional pain that she was intentionally inflicting in an effort to break me in the worst possible way. I knew that she was out to take my soul, and I was certain that she would get it if I was made to endure her own brand of hell for too much longer.

"Rise and shine, Royal," Marta said, breezing into the room like she was a welcome guest.

I quickly closed my eyes to brace for the brightness of the overhead lights. Once I felt their warmth on the skin of my eyelids, I slowly counted to five before finally opening my eyes again and looking up at my capture.

"Why don't you just kill me already?" I mumbled.

"Where would be the fun in that? Besides, this game is just getting started, and I must admit that it's bringing me heights of pleasure that I didn't know existed. Don't you agree?"

I knew that her question was rhetorical, so I didn't even bother trying to formulate a response. My attention and focus were on her and her actions because she still hadn't made it clear why she was gracing me with her presence. For several moments, she stared at me in complete silence, and then, she began to walk a slow circle around the bed I was laying on, checking the chains and handcuffs attached to me. Once she was done making sure that I was secure, she took a seat on the bed and looked down over top of me.

"Your family loves you very much, and they are desperate for your safe return, so I think they will comply with my demands," she said, smiling with self-satisfaction.

"How long do you think that you will live to enjoy whatever it is that you want? Do you really think that we're the type to forgive and forget once you've fucked us over?"

"My sweet Royal, I know that no matter what happens, you will NEVER forget me, and that's just the way that I want it," she replied, inching closer until her lips were but a breath from mine.

At the last second, I averted my head so that her poisonous kiss landed on my cheek. My avoidance didn't deter her actions as her intentions for this visit became clear with the feeling of her lips and tongue doing a slow, seductive crawl down my neck. The vulnerability of being naked for the constant beatings was bad enough, but it still didn't compare to the shame that I felt in these moments. All the love in my heart belonged to Tesha, and yet not even that could convince my body not to respond to Marta's evil seduction. I hated her for what she'd done to me, the betrayal she'd caused of my own body by turning it against me, but even as I thought this, I felt my dick jump with excitement.

As her lips moved down my chest, her hand moved across my thigh until she had my hardening flesh wrapped up in a handshake tighter than a too small condom. The pain that came with every deep breath only heightened my body's senses, and I could feel goosebumps on my skin despite the humid conditions.

"Marta, p-please..."

"Shhh, no begging yet," she replied, moving her hand up and down my shaft with expertise and patience.

In an instant, I was harder than new concrete and more pissed than a caged lion who could smell that his lioness was in heat nearby. When she suddenly stood up and backed away from the bed, I experienced a moment where my senses didn't know which way to go. My body didn't want her to stop, but my mind and soul were wishing for her instant death so that I could relish in her departure from this world. Her brown eyes were locked on mine as she pushed the straps of her purple and yellow sundress off of her shoulders, which caused the light fabric to float to the floor. My best guess had her age at thirty something, but her body was flawless by design, and time had no hold on it. Even if I closed my eyes to deny her beauty, I'd still see her succulent titties, firm, plump ass, and cleanly shaved pussy imprinted on my mind. I could tell by the smile that she was giving me that she knew this truth, and it gave her a twisted pleasure that would continue to feed her as the succubus that she was. When she climbed on top of me and straddled me, I bucked against my restraints in a last-minute effort to avoid my new inevitable, but the chains didn't break.

"This-This doesn't mean anything to me. I don't want you," I said.

"And yet you cum every time," she replied, lowering herself until the head of my dick was trapped within her warm walls.

I held my body completely still, determined not to move, but that just made her laugh out loud.

"Papi, you should know by now that I don't mind doing all the work because it feeds my need to control every aspect of this," she said.

"F-Fuck you!" I growled with anger growing in sync to my dick's rapid throbbing.

"That's the plan, Royal, from now until I get what I want."

The verbal argument ceased the moment that she dropped her full body weight on me and pushed my dick up to the doors of her uterus. The air rushed from my lungs in a painful gasp, and this time when I bucked beneath her, it was involuntary. I could tell by the moan that ripped from her throat that she didn't care though. Pleasure was pleasure as far as she was concerned. Her hands went to my chest, which caused a new wave of pain as she began to ride me like a prized bull at a rodeo. Her pussy's grip was suffocating, making the temperature rise at my core and radiate outward, which caused my skin to redden. No matter how hard I fought against the building desire in me, I still felt its meteoric rise as she alternated between bouncing straight up and down on my dick versus riding it. Stroke after stroke, second after second, I felt my resolve weaken until it finally evaporated, and my back came up off the mattress.

"That's-That's it, Papi. Fuck this pussy like you hate me," she panted, sitting up straight so that she could grab her titties and play with her nipples.

I did my best to ignore the sound of her voice, just so that I could fully concentrate on getting her to climax. Past experience had taught me that if I fucked her like she wanted, then the sex would last for maybe one or two rounds, but if I held out, then she could go all night long. I'd never known the word insatiable until I'd had this woman on my dick because she knew how to ride a muthafucka until his shit hurt. She was possessed by an idea that no amount of logical reasoning could sway, and that kept me at her mercy.

"Keep it-Keep it going," she demanded, riding me fast enough for the sounds of our skin slapping to echo off of the walls.

The familiar grip of her pussy pulsating let me know that she was seconds away from fulfillment, which meant that it was time for me to deploy my secret weapon. I closed my eyes and let my imagination run wild with memories of Tesha from our wedding night when we'd made love all over our castle. Only through this imagery and the reliving of these sacred moments was I able to cum, and I prayed for forgiveness the entire time that my dick was spewing semen inside of Marta. She continued to ride me through the wave of her own orgasm, only stopping once she was completely spent and exhausted. My lungs felt like they were on fire, and my ribs hurt bad enough to make me cry, but I would never give this bitch that type of satisfaction.

"Get off me," I ordered, not even trying to mask the disgust in my tone.

"It's okay. You know how much I hate to cuddle," she replied, chuckling as she climbed off of me and moved to put her dress back on.

I did my best not to watch her, but I was still very much aware of her body out of the corner of my eye. Part of me knew that if I learned to play along better, then I could probably manipulate her into letting her guard down, but it was a tough pill to swallow. It would also take a lot of finesse because she would undoubtedly be suspicious if I suddenly changed my tune of hatred that I'd been singing to her. Something had to change though because this was about survival, and the fact that my family hadn't gotten me out of this mess yet signaled that I needed to learn to help myself when opportunities presented themselves.

"Marta, we can't keep doing this."

She turned around to look at me while still stuffing her titties back inside her dress.

"Of course we can. You are a young, virile man, Royal, and your dick gets hard with little to no motivation from me. We can do this for however long we need to," she replied, smiling at me.

"That's not what I mean. We can't keep doing this because the beatings from your men are fucking me up, and I'm not healed before they want to go another round. I may be young and strong, but any human body can only take so much."

My words caused her to go silent in thought, but I could see that she was actually considering what I was saying.

"It sounds like you're asking me to trust you by letting you regain your full strength. Is that what this is?" she asked, giving me a quizzical look.

"No, I'm telling you to make it make sense. You want my body, but you allow your men to keep fucking me up for no reason, which is messing with your own agenda. All I'm asking you to do is think it through."

I'd learned long ago that the best tactic of manipulation was to make the person think that what you really wanted to happen was their idea. This created a dance of sorts, but with the mind instead of the body.

"If I agree to this, do you agree to help me with my goals?"

"That's not what I'm saying either. I'm simply pointing out that there's no way that you get everything that you want if I'm dead. You're a boss, right? So think that shit all the way through because, right now, you're doing everything except keeping me drugged up so you can remove my kidney," I said.

Her smirk gave me a confident feeling that I'd passed the slick little test that she'd tried to throw at me by trying to trick me into an obvious lie. The moment that I said that I agreed to the dumb shit, she would've discounted everything else I had to say, and we both knew that. So I stuck to the truth, and now, I just had to resist the urge to do my best job of selling her something she wasn't trying to buy. She continued to stare at me, but her thoughts were very much an unknown at this point, so I didn't know which way she was leaning in her decision. After a few moments, she walked from the room without a word, leaving the light on, which normally signaled the next phase of the torture cycle. Sleep deprivation was an easy way to fuck with people's minds and force them to make a choice between submission or deterioration into psychosis. I'd only heard of these tactics of warfare until I'd become an unintended guest of the Red Devil, but now, I could attest to their effectiveness. In my moments of delirium, I saw Tesha's face and the face of my late mother. One gave me hope while the other inspired fear because I felt like seeing my mother signaled how close I was to being reunited with her through death. As badly as I missed my mom, I knew that it wasn't my time yet. I closed my eyes and tried to center myself in preparation of whatever was next to come, and by the time I heard approaching footsteps, I was as ready as I could be.

"Does it hurt when you sit up?" Marta asked.

My eyes immediately snapped open to find her standing over me with a plate in her hand. The tantalizing aromas wafting off of the food on the plate made my stomach growl in angry resentment mixed with excitement, but I kept my cool.

"Yes, it hurts because my ribs are broken."

She nodded once, and then, she sat down beside me on the bed.

"I tried not to make it too hot," she said, scooping up a forkful of beans and rice, which she carefully guided into my mouth.

I couldn't stop my eyes from closing in satisfaction or stop the moan that rumbled through my chest. I forced myself to chew slowly in order to savor every morsel of flavor, and surprisingly, she waited patiently before feeding me another bite of food.

"Why are you doing this?" I asked.

"Because it makes sense. I need you strong physically, even if you are weak mentally, so I will nurse you back to health myself. This will ensure that you're able to get me pregnant."

Chapter 4

(David)

The sense of déjà vu that I felt as soon as my eyes opened brought both relief and pain. I felt relief at still being alive after getting shot again, but the pain came from seeing Tynesha asleep beside my hospital bed. So much had happened, and most of it had been bad shit, since the last time that I'd awoken in a Miami hospital with my wife nowhere in sight. Back then though, I'd known that I had her love even when I couldn't see her face, but now, I was so confused about my life in this moment that I honestly didn't know what to think. Up until the moment I'd stepped in front of the bullet for Ty, I'd thought that I hated her with every part of my soul, but now I questioned how that could be true. If I did, in fact, hate her then I would've allowed Shaomi to put a few slugs in her, and I would've delighted in watching her disappear into the afterlife. I didn't do that though. Without conscious thought, I'd instinctively protected Ty, and somewhere in the back of my mind, I knew that the only reason I'd done it was out of love.

Whether it was love for her or for our kids, I didn't know yet, but that was something that I'd have to figure out sooner than later.

"How are you feeling?" Carrie whispered, causing me to shift my gaze to the other side of the bed.

I gave her a nonverbal response by slowly pointing to my chest where I could still feel the hole that the hot slug left.

"I've never had the pleasure, but I've heard that it hurts like a big bitch," she whispered.

I cracked a smile and gave a slight nod just as I saw that Ty started stirring out of the corner of my eye. When I looked back at her, those hazel green eyes were alert and locked on my face with an intensity that made my breathing change gears. She didn't immediately speak, but it was obvious to me that there was so much that she wanted to say.

"I'm gonna step out to see if I can find a vending machine because my stomach is growling," Carrie said, hopping up and heading for the door.

Neither of us spoke or acknowledged Carrie in any way. We just continued our silent staring contest. After a few moments, I had to acknowledge within myself that my ego was getting in the way of me breaking the ice, and there was too much at stake for that.

"Come here," I said in a voice that sounded like new sandpaper.

The hesitation was clear to see in her eyes, but when I patted the spot on my bed beside me, she slowly got up and moved to it. The familiar scent of her body invaded my senses and sent immediate signals to my memories that I had to fight against because now wasn't the time for that. Now wasn't even the time to celebrate me surviving the latest brush with death that I'd had because my kids were still in danger, and that was unacceptable.

"Talk to me, Ty."

"And say what? I don't know what to say to you anymore," she confessed, swallowing the tears in her throat.

"Just start from the beginning of the end."

I could tell by the flash of fear that illuminated her eyes that she knew the exact moment in time that I was referring to but talking about it wouldn't be easy. For a few moments, she simply stared off into space, but I was content to let her take her time to form the words needed.

"The way that Shaomi was talking and acting during that last video call was weird as fuck, but I couldn't figure out what game she was playing. My mind was focused on sending you an S.O.S. message for help without alerting Roland to what was going on, and it was hard because he was sitting right there. All that I kept on thinking was that I needed to keep him calm in order to keep me and the baby alive, so I did the only thing that I could think of. I convinced him that the baby was his. I never thought in a million years that you would believe that lie, but based on how it was presented to you, I kinda understand now. Shaomi's mission was to destroy our family and take you back from me. We all played into her hands," she said softly, shaking her head in disbelief mixed with regret.

Without a doubt, I knew that the blame in this situation was both of ours, but it took a moment of true self-reflection to formulate my own words.

"It was fucked up of me to sleep with your sister and mom, and I make no excuses for any of it. I make no excuses for Shaomi either because I should've seen through her bullshit intentions from the day when you pulled a gun on her in our apartment. I was just on some fuck nigga shit," I confessed honestly.

"Yeah, you were... but I didn't have to play that game with you, and especially not with Roland. I wanted to hurt you, or destroy you if I could, and even though you deserved my hate, that move was beneath me. I'm not saying that I forgive you for it all, but I'm woman enough to admit that I could've handled shit better too."

The fact that she was now looking at me as she spoke allowed me to gauge the sincerity behind her words, and what I saw brought a little closure to the hole in my heart.

"Tell me about the kids," I said, reaching for her hand.

She allowed our fingers to interlock, but I could still feel the enormous amount of tension in her body radiating down through her fingertips.

"I had no idea that I was pregnant with twins. I thought that I was just carrying your daughter, even though I was lying to Roland and saying it was a boy. Well, the day that I went into labor, I was by myself in the hospital for a while, and I was able to convince the doctors and nurses that it wasn't healthy for me to have people in the room while I was giving birth.

"I took this precaution just in case Roland somehow found out that I was in labor because I didn't want him there. Secretly, you're the only person that I wanted by my side. Your son, Rashon, was delivered first, and I thought that was the only surprise for the day, but a few minutes later, your daughter made her grand entrance..."

"And then what happened?" I asked after she'd paused in speech.

"I panicked. All I could think about was the impossibility of being able to run away from Roland with two kids, so I knew that I had to protect our daughter. I explained part of my situation to the nurse and convinced her to save our daughter's life by taking her far away. I have no idea where she went to. I only know her name because I vowed to find her once it was safe to do so. I know that you probably think I'm a bad mom, but, David, I..."

"I don't think that. I know that you did the best that you could to keep them both safe, and you shouldn't have had to do that on your own because I should've been there," I said, squeezing her hand tightly.

Her eyes immediately filled up with tears, and there was no dam in place to keep them from free falling down her cheeks. The sadness that I saw in her only added bricks to the mansion of guilt that my actions had constructed, but all I wanted in this moment was to take away her pain. I was her husband, her protector, and I'd failed miserably at both jobs.

"We'll find our daughter. I promise. Tell me about Rashon though," I said.

"Marta has him. She won't give him back to me unless we somehow break somebody out of prison for her and then either serve up Royal's kid or kill Royal's kid. Which means killing your daughter."

I could see the distaste as she spoke about the child that was biologically mine and her twin sister's, but I couldn't fault her for how she felt. I just couldn't let that be important right now.

"Did she give you the information on who needs to be broken out and what prison they're in?" I asked.

"No, but I can get it. I think that she has just been giving me time to find you and speak with Royal's family."

"Why would you speak to Royal's family?" I asked, confused.

"Because Marta has Royal held hostage somewhere in that building, and she's not turning him loose until the demands are met."

This piece of information added to the mathematical equation in my mind, and it was tougher to digest than trigonometry.

"Marta is trying to force us to work together," I stated.

"The same way that you and Royal worked together the night that you hit her house chasing Viktor. She told me about it and how you told Royal to spare both her and her son."

"Yeah, I did, but he told me why you didn't spare anyone, and it looks like he was right because this shit has come back to haunt us," I replied, feeling anger build within myself.

"So, what do we do, bae? How do we get out of this without sacrificing the life of someone we love?"

Her question was a fair one mixed with extreme complications and variables beyond our control, but it was the way that she asked it that had me looking at her strangely.

"You called me bae," I said.

"You took a bullet for me, and I guess that made me a little bit sentimental, but don't let it go to your head because I need you to stay focused."

Her tone was serious, but I could see the smile that she was holding back. I wouldn't call her on it right now, but it would definitely come back up at a later date.

"Okay, I'm focused. Marta has Royal and Rashon. Before I got shot, you were saying that you never attacked my compound or kidnapped Uncle Umar, so I don't know who..."

"It was Tesha. Carrie and I figured that out," she said, screwing her face up in obvious anger.

I didn't argue or offer any counter opinion because it all made too much sense now that she'd actually said it, and I knew that I probably should've seen it sooner.

"She's been keeping my daughter away from me, so I can't exactly say that I'm surprised. If she harms my uncle, I'm gonna kill her. I just wanna be honest with you about that."

"I hear you on that, but for real, I don't think that's her plan. I mean, she could've killed him right then and there, and the fact that she didn't means that she thinks he's valuable or useful," Ty said.

"So, do you think that she knows about Royal and is planning to use my uncle to force me to help?" I asked.

"That's a thought. Or it could be as simple as her taking Umar off of the board because her and her hittas were planning to make another run at you and Shaomi on your own turf."

"Well, whatever her motivations were don't really matter at this point because we all have to work together or risk losing someone that we love," I said.

The nod that she gave me was resigned and defeated, but when I squeezed her hand, she squeezed mine right back. All of a sudden, the hospital door opened soundlessly, and Carrie poked her head inside.

"You two ain't bout to have a shootout, are you?" she asked.

"Bitch, please. I'm still healing from the last round," Ty replied.

"Wait, you got shot too?" I asked, immediately concerned.

"Don't let her hype that shit up, David, because the bullet just barely made it inside of her left shoulder, and traveling through your thick ass chest is what slowed it down," Carrie said, coming all the way into the room and sitting back down.

"Did you get stitches?" I asked.

In response to my question, Ty pulled down her shirt so that I could see the fresh wound and stitches right below her collarbone.

"You can say whatever the fuck you wanna say, but that .45 wasn't no bitch," Ty stated.

"You ain't never lied," I agreed, still feeling the pain my damn self.

"Awww, poor babies," Carrie replied mockingly.

Me and Ty both flipped her the middle finger, which made her laugh out loud. For a few seconds, everything seemed as normal as when we were in Florida, but a sudden thought shattered that illusion for me.

"How bad is Shaomi hurt?" I asked, looking over at Carrie.

The blank stare that she gave me would've been comical under different circumstances, but right now it filled me with trepidation.

"David..." Ty said, squeezing my hand to get my attention.

When I looked back to her, I understood immediately what Carrie had been struggling to say, but I didn't know how to feel yet.

"She's dead, huh?" I asked softly.

"Yeah, and I'm really sorry, David," Carrie replied immediately.

"No, Carrie, we're not doing that. Enough lies have been told, and I refuse to let this be another one," Ty said.

"I don't understand," I said, looking from one woman to the next, confused.

"Ty, are you sure about this?" Carrie asked.

Ty nodded, and then, she turned fully to face me while wrapping her other hand around the one she already had entwined with mine. I had no idea what she was about to say, but it was obviously important and serious.

"David, Shaomi is dead, but Carrie didn't kill her. I did."

For a second, I just stared at her as I waited on her words to compute and ultimately trigger the right emotional response.

"I don't understand," I repeated.

"I shot her and killed her because I couldn't accept that she stood to gain from all of the destruction that she'd caused," Ty explained.

"Okay... I can understand that, but I don't understand why I don't feel anything about what you just told me. I mean, she was pregnant with my child, so shouldn't I feel some sense of loss for that at least?"

"You're probably just numb to it right now," Ty replied.

"Or maybe somewhere in the back of your mind, you always knew that Shaomi was a villain in your movie of life and therefore undeserving of your sympathy," Carrie said.

"Damn, bitch, did you just go there?" Ty asked, visibly surprised by Carrie's candor.

I wasn't surprised though because the relationship that I had with Carrie only worked when we were brutally honest with each other. I needed that from her, and this exact moment was a good example of why because her words forced me to not run from the truth that was within myself.

"I appreciate you telling me the truth, Ty, but I can't worry about the stages of grief right now. We've gotta save our kids and kill Marta once and for all."

Chapter 5

(Tynesha) (Mexico City – Two Days Later)

The confidence that I felt when I walked into Marta's high rise building this time around reminded me of who I used to be, and it made me wonder if the change was having David back on my side. While I had no illusions that we were miraculously the happy couple that had swam through the mud in Florida, I did know for certain that he had my back. His kids meant the world to him, just like they did to me, and that was the foundation that we stood on in this moment. Now, it was time to stand on business.

I crossed through the lobby with purposeful strides, allowing the sounds of my six-inch, thigh high, Black Billionaire stiletto boots to turn heads, along with the natural sway of my hips in my black leggings. My eyes were hidden behind my Dolce and Gabana frames, but they were scanning everything and everyone like two searchlights crisscrossing a prison yard. I could tell by the way the cute Latina behind the desk watched me intently that it was a safe bet that she had a gun in her hand, but I kept moving straight toward the bank of elevators.

When I got there, one of Marta's minions was waiting for me with a Draco clutched in his grip and a mean mug on his face. Outwardly, I knew that I looked poised and nonchalant, but on the inside, my stomach was in knots because I knew that I needed to keep all of my emotions in check for the sake of my son. As we took the elevator ride up, I worked on keeping my breathing at a normal rate and checking all the urges that I had to choke a bitch. A few minutes later, I was led into her penthouses apartment where I found her sitting on the couch, sipping slowly from a glass of champagne.

"Buenos días. Can I offer you a drink?" she asked.

"Nah, I'm good."

As she continued indulging in her beverage, her eyes did a slow, thorough assessment of me from head to toe. She didn't voice her thoughts, but she did nothing to hide the curiosity swimming in her eyes.

"So, on the phone, you said that you needed information, but something tells me that you did not come all this way for that which you could've easily gotten during our call. What is it that you really want?" she asked.

"Well, first, I need to know who we're breaking out and where exactly are we breaking him out from. I also need proof of life for my son and for Royal too."

"And you would not trust me to send you these things over the phone? I thought that we had a better understanding than that," she replied, feigning like my distrust actually wounded her.

The smirk that popped up on my face was genuine, but I had to bite my tongue in order to not add a scathing reply to go along with it. The silence hung for a moment between us before she sat her glass down, stood up, and left the room. I waited a few seconds and then made sure that the movement of sticking my hands into the pockets of my leather jacket that I was wearing was natural in case I was being watched. I took a seat on the couch and pretended to be adjusting my boot while carefully placing the listening device that I'd gotten from one of Umar's militia under the coffee table in front of me. I got it secured and just had time to sit back before Marta came around the corner with Rashon in her arms. I could tell that he'd been asleep because his little chubby fists were rubbing at his eyes, but as soon as he saw me, his eyes lit up with excitement. The squeal that escaped his mouth brought me so much joy and tore my heart out all at the same time.

"Hey, fat man! How's my fat baby?" I asked, holding my arms out wide to him.

Before Marta even got to me, Rashon was leaning like he intended to jump out of her arms if she didn't hurry the fuck up. The pain in my shoulder was ignored as I pulled my son to me and took the deepest breath of my life. Rashon was just jabbering away with baby talk, but I couldn't respond through the tears that I couldn't stop from rolling down my cheeks. In my mind, I had to keep telling myself not to freak out and not to let my emotions take over me, or I might lose him forever. For me to lose control was what Marta wanted but knowing that didn't make it any easier to maintain the composure that I'd worked so hard to craft on my way here. I drew all the strength that I could from my baby boy, and then, I gave him kisses from me and his daddy like David had asked of me.

"I'll be back for you soon, fat man. You be good," I whispered in his ear.

When I looked up, Marta was standing almost on top of us, wearing a smug expression that I wanted to shoot off of her face with several bullets. I was determined not to give her the satisfaction of seeing just how painful this was for me, which was part of the reason that I'd worn oversized sunglasses. My tears had somewhat been absorbed by my son's shirt, but even if she knew that I was crying, I still didn't have to let her feed off of me. I spotted Abuela standing a little past Marta with a bottle in her hand, and I knew that was the perfect distraction for the moment.

"Would you like to feed him?" Marta offered.

I knew that her generosity was fake as fuck, and there wasn't a chance in hell that I was going to give her more control in this moment. Instead, I stood up with him in my arms and took him to Abuela. I kissed him once more on the forehead while saying a silent prayer to God for him to watch over my baby, and then, I transferred him into the other woman's arms. He immediately started to fuss, but the bottle quickly captured his attention, and I was allowed to quietly back away. It killed me though, and it made me want to kill both of these bitches with my bare hands. I was barely able to resist the temptation as I turned back around to face Marta.

"Now take me to Royal," I demanded.

The smugness of her expression only faltered a little, but it was enough to create more emotional stability within myself. Without a word, she turned and led the way down the hall, farther into her penthouse, until we came to a closed bedroom door at the end of the hall. When she opened the door, I had to fight not to gag because of the odor that came leaping out of the darkness like every boogie man in a scary movie. The smell of blood was the dominant aroma, but unless my mind was playing tricks on me, I could've sworn that I smelled old sex in the air. Marta flipped a switch, and the overhead lights came on, and then she led me into the room. Royal was laid out on a blood soaked, dingy mattress, naked as the day that he came into this world, chained and handcuffed. His eyes were closed, and it looked like he wasn't breathing, which sent a chill of fear up my spine because I knew that his death would directly affect the chances of me saving my son's life.

"Did you kill him slow or just fuck him to death?" I asked.

The look that Marta threw at me over her shoulder was one of anger and annoyance, but she didn't say a word. Instead, she sat beside Royal on the bed and slowly traced one of the still healing cuts across his chest with her index finger. His eyes snapped open, and they were alert, which restored the little bit of hope that I'd lost a few seconds before.

"You've got a visitor," Marta said, looking over at me.

When his eyes rolled upward in my direction, the first emotion that took hold of him was pure panic, and I heard the rattle of his chains as he struggled to free himself.

"T-Tesha, baby, why did you come..."

"I'm not Tesha, nigga," I replied, lowering my shades enough for him to see my eyes.

I could tell that he didn't believe me at first, but then, the light in his eyes dimmed considerably, and I knew that he'd realized the truth.

"This is the friend that you came to see, no?" she asked with a slick smile.

"Only we know that's not true, right, Royal?" I asked.

He didn't respond, but he didn't really have to because the pieces of the puzzle already fit together in my mind.

"You have your proof of life, so what now?" she asked.

I pulled my phone out and took a few quick photos of them on the bed before returning the phone to my pocket.

"Now you tell me who we're breaking out of prison," I replied.

"Does-Does my family know that I'm here?" he asked, looking directly at me.

"Yeah, they know," I replied shortly.

I could feel that he wanted to ask me about Tesha, but he wisely kept his mouth shut on that topic. I, on the other hand, wanted some clarity about one issue.

"Humor me, Royal, and tell me if it was your idea or Tesha's to come after me and my son," I said.

"It was mine," he replied without hesitation.

I didn't respond, but I smiled down at him knowingly because his lie was very transparent.

"Anything else?" Marta asked.

"Nah, I've seen enough. You might want to give him a bath though because the smell of old pussy is not a fragrance that ages well in the heat," I replied, chuckling as I turned and stepped back out of the room.

I heard Marta whisper something to him, and then, she followed me out while making sure the door was shut behind us. I walked back up the hallway with her to the living room, and my mind was moving at hyper speed, trying to plan my next move.

"The man that you must break out is named Felipe Sandoval," Marta said.

"Are you sure that you want to break him out? I mean, you seem to be having a lot of fun with Royal's dick," I replied.

"Is it your goal to anger me by speaking about shit that you know nothing about? If so, then continue with your current line of questioning."

The threat in her tone was clear, and even though I had my gun on me, I knew the wisdom in keeping shit cute. For now.

"Where is this Felipe being held?" I asked.

"I don't know his location, only that he's in a prison in the United States somewhere."

"Uh, that's like looking for a needle in a stack of needles. You've gotta give me more information because I would like to have my son back before his eighteenth birthday," I replied sarcastically with mounting frustration.

"He was arrested two years ago in Texas, accused of murder, drug trafficking, racketeering, and conspiracy. No one has heard from him since."

"So, how do you even know that he's still alive? For all you know, he could've hung himself because he was looking at so much time. Or his associates could've killed him to keep him silent," I said.

"He is El Jefe of the Zeta Cartel, and no one associated with him would dare harm him. And I know that he would never commit suicide because he wouldn't do that to his daughter."

"You two have a daughter?" I asked, somewhat surprised.

"I am his daughter."

Her revelation surprised me, but now the lengths that she was willing to go made a lot more sense. A girl's daddy was her first love. When I looked over at Marta, I was seeing her through a different lens, but it didn't make my hate for her lessen. It only made me understand her a little.

"We'll find him, and we'll get him back to you, but you better uphold your end of the bargain. If not, you both die, and that's a promise," I stated.

Her nod was enough of a response for me, and I left her standing right where she was as I walked out of her apartment. On the ride down in the elevator, I pulled my phone to check for signal strength, but as expected, I got a whole lot of nothing, so I put it away. This building wasn't nearly as formidable as the one we'd lived in back in Orlando, but being able to take control of it by assault before my son died would be impossible. On my trip back across the lobby, I kept my eyes in motion with the same amount of knowledge gathering energy as when I came in, taking my time the whole way.

By the time I stepped out into the midmorning air, I had a count of the visible cameras between the lobby and the elevators, along with a memory imprinted of how the chick looked behind the desk. The two Lincoln town cars that I'd arrived with were still idling front and center in front of the building, courtesy of their diplomatic plates and the four men standing around them clutching AR-15s. One man opened the door of the second car for me to get in the back of, but suddenly, my steps faltered as I got a strange sensation of being watched. There was no doubt that Marta's people were watching me and the hittas I'd come with, but this didn't feel like that. This feeling of being watched came with a threat so real that I slid my hand inside of my leather jacket and wrapped it around the butt of my Glock .40 in my shoulder holster. When I got to the Lincoln, I stopped and looked around nice and slow at everything and everyone moving in front of me.

At first, no one looked out of place, but then, I saw her standing across the street in front of a bank. Even at this distance, I knew exactly who it was because her face was as familiar to me as my own, due to the fact that we were identical twins. I'd had no contact with Tesha, so I had no idea what she was doing here. In my mind, I understood that I had to keep shit cool and keep it cute because we all had a position to play, but my heart responded before my mind could get full control of my actions. Before I knew it, my gun was out, and my finger was on the trigger, squeezing twice with each breath I took. I was out for blood.

Chapter 6

(Tesha)

"Okay, so what's the plan?" I asked, looking across the table at Angel and Destiny.

We were all sitting in a booth in a little breakfast café across from the building where we believed that Royal was still being held. For the past few mornings, we posted up in this exact spot, watching the foot traffic going in and out of the building, while assessing it for points of weakness. None of us had ventured inside of the tall glass structure yet, so we didn't know what it looked like inside, but there were plenty of goons with guns roaming around outside. I thought that it would've been easy to get a look inside because of the building's design, but the glass had some type of tint to it that made it impenetrable. We would be flying blind as soon as we walked through the door.

"I'm still trying to get the building's blueprints, but it's literally been a dead end at every turn because there's no official documentation about the architectural design or the designer. It's like a ghost built that bitch," Destiny said, looking clearly frustrated.

"You know that the cartels are known for making a muthafucka disappear after they build the drug pipelines across the border, so do you really think that they won't kill a nigga after that?" Angel asked, pointing to the luxury high rise in question.

"I feel you, sis, but damn, they would've had to take out whole construction crews," Destiny said, shaking her head.

"What's the latest word from FatherGod?" I asked.

"I ain't talked to him in a few days, but Madeline told me that he's been spending hours at you and Royal's house at the gun range, shooting," Angel replied, her forehead creasing in concern.

"With all the guns and shit Royal has collected there, I'm sure that he'll be occupied for a while," I said.

"I wouldn't bet on that. If I know our dad, I'd say that shooting at paper targets is old already, and he's thirsty to shed blood sooner than later," Destiny stated.

This prediction only increased the worry on Angel's face, but we'd already had the discussion about it only being a matter of time before Jonathan "FatherGod" Walker came out of retirement for good. Our decision to stay in Mexico had been a hard sell because, truthfully, my father-in-law had wanted to erase Mexico in a permanent way. I knew that he had pull with the Russian president, who had bombs at his fingertips, but the fact that we knew Royal was down here somewhere kept everyone's fingers off of nuclear devices.

"We need to put a plan together," I said, breathing a sigh of frustration myself as I pushed the remaining food on my plate away.

When I looked out of the window back toward the building we'd been staking out, I saw something new and interesting.

"When did those cars pull up?" I asked, nodding toward the two all black Lincolns.

Both women's eyes slid in the direction of the building, and it was clear that this was the first time that they'd noticed them too.

"I don't know, but those are definitely diplomatic plates," Destiny replied, pulling her phone out.

"There ain't no way that you can read that plate from here," Angel said.

"I don't have to read it in order to know that it's a diplomatic plate because those are easy enough to recognize. What I'm doing now is hacking into the Mexican consulate to backdoor my way into their foreign affairs database so that I can find out what diplomat is in town. If we know who that is, then we may be able to leverage that," Destiny explained as her fingers danced across her phone's screen. I nodded because I was listening, but my eyes remained locked across the street in case someone recognizable came out. The men standing around holding big guns was a sure sign that whoever it was traveling behind those diplomatic tinted windows had power, money, or both. To me, that meant that they WERE the leverage.

"I'mma get a better look," I said, sliding out of the booth and heading for the front door.

Neither woman tried to stop me or did anything to indicate that they were coming with me, but I felt comfortable knowing that I had my gun on me just in case something happened. I didn't want to be so obvious as to cross the street to walk along the same side as the activity I was observing, but I had to be sure that I got a clear look at whoever the person or people in charge were. I walked slowly down my side of the street, stopping in front of a bank that was almost directly across from the high-rise building. My intuition told me that it wasn't safe to stand here for too long because I didn't need to stick out on some weird shit. I kept my eyes moving though, just to make sure that I was staying aware of my surroundings.

The people who were out and about were obviously business types, based on their attire and the stiff body language of someone working a nine to five that slowly killed more of their soul each day. I was completely ignored as people moved around and past me, but I was okay with that. After standing in the same spot for about five minutes, I knew that it was time to move again, but just as I did, I saw the front door to the high rise building open. In my mind, there was no particular person that I expected to see emerge, but I damn sure hadn't thought that my twin was the woman responsible for the armed motorcade. At first, I thought that I was tripping, but the way that the men with guns, who'd been posted around the cars, suddenly went on high alert around her confirmed my belief. The question was what the fuck was Tynesha doing coming out of that building, free as a bird, while my husband was trapped?

Impulsively, I wanted to cross the street and ask her muthafuckin ass with my gun down her throat, but I waited to see if a better alternative popped into my mind. My eyes stayed locked on her though, and then, suddenly, she was looking up at me in a direct way that dispelled any notion I had of not being seen. I couldn't see her eyes behind her shades, so I couldn't quite read her facial expression, but when she pulled her gun, I knew that her thoughts had murderous intent. I dove to my right seconds before the glass of the bank's front facing picture window shattered behind me, and then, the air was filled with screams of panic. I knew not to stay on the ground out in the open, so I kept rolling to the left while reaching for my own gun to return fire. I was shooting blindly in Ty's direction as I got up and ran toward the café.

Before I could pull the door open to dive inside, the door swung outward, and Destiny stepped into the daylight with her gun in her grip howling bullets at Ty. Angel was right behind her, shooting too. Their cover fire allowed me to regroup so that I could turn around and take aim, but by the time I did that, Ty had vanished into one of the cars that was speeding away.

"Get to the Jeep!" I yelled, already sprinting toward the parking lot on the side of the building.

We all hopped in, and Destiny had us fishtailing out onto the main street in hot pursuit of the fast-fleeing town cars. By the time we got within three car lengths of them, I had my gun out the window with bullets blowing from the barrel like trained skydivers. Seeing the back window of the second car shatter into dust filled me with adrenaline that I could taste mixed with my saliva, and it was motivation for me to keep firing. The dry click of my empty clip was the instant karma I faced for my growing excitement over the hunt, but I wasn't discouraged.

"I need a gun," I said, reaching toward Destiny in the driver's seat.

She quickly pushed her stainless-steel Ruger .45 into my hand without taking her eyes off of the road, and then, I was back out the window, airing that bitch out. We were gaining on them when, suddenly, a Mexican police SUV slammed into the front quarter panel of the Jeep, sending us into a wild spin. I inadvertently dropped the gun that I had been shooting out the window because I was forced to either hold onto the door or go flying out into traffic my damn self. The Jeep spun two full times before tilting precariously on two wheels and almost flipping us upside down, but then, it dropped back to the ground.

"Man, what the fuck?" Angel groaned.

"Are you two hurt?" Destiny asked.

"Nah, I'm good, but them muthafuckas ain't hit us on no damn accident," I said, sitting up and rubbing my neck.

"I think you're right, T. Just don't make any sudden moves and raise your hands nice and slow," Destiny said.

I was confused by what she was telling me to do until I looked out of the window and saw that we were surrounded by angry Mexicans holding AK-47s. The expressions on their faces easily said that they had no problem spraying our brains all over the pavement, and I damn sure wasn't about to play with that type of energy. I followed Destiny's instructions and raised my hands nice and slow, and after a few seconds, they advanced on us to pull us out of the Jeep.

"What did we do?" I asked in Spanish.

The man who had grabbed my arm to pull me out said not a word but instead hit me with a backhand slap so vicious that my head bounced off the side of the Jeep, which caused my vision to swim. I didn't have time to recover before he was dragging me to another SUV, but I was smart enough to keep my mouth shut this time. He slapped a pair of cuffs on me and then shoved me into the back of the SUV with considerable force. I didn't know where Angel and Destiny were because we immediately pulled off, and I resisted the urge to ask the question that would probably cost me to pay in blood the next time around.

Right about now was the moment in time when I remembered the infamous line from every cop show about my right to remain silent because I needed to exercise that bitch to the max. There was one man in the backseat with me and two up front, including the driver, but none of them spoke a word. It was my hope that I could figure out what the fuck was going on through eavesdropping on what they had to say, but so far that shit was getting me nothing except for more frustration.

We rode in silence for twenty minutes, and all I could think about was the fact that my slippery ass twin had cheated death one more time. I didn't just want her dead though. I wanted all the answers that she had when it came to my husband and what his current condition was. She had the truth, which could only buy her so much time because FatherGod wanted the same answers that I did. The illusion in my mind of us being able to talk like grown women who loved each other had shattered like the bank's window when Ty had tried to knock my head off. Now, I knew that only one of us would be left standing, and I was determined that it would be me.

When we pulled up to the police station, I was unceremoniously dragged out and hauled inside. I thought that I would've been taken to some musty interrogation room where I'd ask the routine questions for my lawyer and my phone call, but instead, I was pulled by the back of my neck into the back of the station and thrown in a cell. In order to avoid a swan dive into a toilet full of shit, piss, and blood, I had to run headfirst into a wall and bounce back up like a Jack in the Box.

Without a doubt, I was headed for a concussion, but I managed not to fall or land on the two angry looking Spanish women sitting on the steel bench against the opposite wall. In rapid Spanish, the cop told me to hurry up and put my back to the gate or he would leave the cuffs on me for the night, so I did as I was told. With the cold metal removed from my wrists, I didn't feel quite as vulnerable, but I knew that I wouldn't feel anything reasonably safe until Angel and Destiny arrived. Being locked up with allies was better than being alone any day. There was room for me to sit down beside the other two women, but the looks on their faces were none too welcoming, so I stayed put.

"What you in for?" the shorter of the two asked in English.

"Speeding," I replied in Spanish.

"Chica, you can drop the Spanglish that you're butchering because your accent sucks, and you're clearly American. Secondly, you don't get thrown in the back for speeding, especially not if you're American, so do you wanna try again?" she asked.

The smartass in me had two responses ready to fly off of the tip of my tongue, but I had to weigh the consequences of popping shit right now.

"All I know is that I was shooting at somebody, and then the cops ran into my Jeep," I replied, using clear English this time.

"You were shooting at someone... in Mexico City?" she asked slowly.

When I nodded, she looked left to her companion, and then they both burst out laughing.

"You wanna let me in on the joke?" I asked with sarcastic frustration building.

"The joke is that you would be so stupid to come this far away from home to do something so completely dumb. With the way you're dressed, I'm sure you don't have the type of money that it will take to bribe the cops and judges out here, so unless you have some very powerful friends, chica, you're fucked. Literally," she said, smiling unsympathetically.

"What do you mean, literally?" I asked.

"Well, with no money and no friends, your pussy is the only thing that will keep you alive and fed in our prison system. I hope it's good," she replied, snickering.

I kept my facial expression neutral, but the panic that I felt was as real as the cramps in my stomach right now. I could lie to these bitches straight to their faces, but in my heart, I knew that I wasn't bout that life of fucking and sucking to survive. I'd rather die first, but the thought of that crushed me because I knew what it would do to my daughter. There had to be another way out though because my husband had long money, which meant that I had long money too.

"Who do I gotta bribe?" I asked seriously.

"I mean, you could try to bribe me, but I'm really not into that sort of thing, and it's only gonna add to your list of charges," a man said from behind me.

I turned around to find a middle-aged, white man with sandy brown hair in a blue sports coat and some black slacks standing at the bars a few feet away. I'd never met him before, but his accent was definitely American and completely southern.

"Who are you?" I asked in a guarded tone.

"Me? Well, you can just consider me your personal chauffeur until I get you home," he replied with a smile.

"I'm-I'm going home?" I asked, feeling the immediate rush of excitement fill my chest.

"Oh, yeah, of course. The great state of Texas is welcoming you with open arms on the count of capital murder. Are you ready to go?"

IMMA DIE BOUT MINE 5 | ARYANNA

Chapter 7

(Royal)

Ever since I'd seen Tynesha's face, my mind had been racing nonstop, analyzing and reanalyzing what her presence signified and how I needed to proceed next. A proof of life demand meant that my family was definitely involved because Ty could give two fucks if I was dead or alive considering the fact that I'd come all this way to kill her. This knowledge gave me something to use as motivation when it came to enduring my circumstances, but I was also afraid of what Tesha would think when she saw the pictures of me. Would she automatically think that I'd been fucking Marta because I was naked, or would it be because Ty told her that she smelled the sins of sex in the air? For there to be an expectation of compassion from Ty would've been stupid on my part, which meant that I needed to figure out what I was going to say when I had the chance to see my wife again.

"I can tell that you're in deep thought because you didn't even hear me walk up on you," Marta said.

When I looked up, she was standing right beside me with a plate of food in her hands and a blank expression on her face.

"I guess that you could say that. Ty showing back up here means some type of progress is being made, but I don't know exactly what that means because you ain't told me a whole lot."

She continued to look down at me in silence for a few moments before finally taking a seat beside me on the bed. I could tell that she wanted to say something, but she was either struggling to find the words or hesitant to use them for whatever reason. I could wait though because it wasn't like I had a choice or any other options.

"Ty didn't just come to see you. She came for proof of life of her son as well because I've decided to keep him until my demands are met. I needed everyone involved to be sufficiently motivated to carry out the necessary tasks because it won't be easy. She also needed the name and location of the man who must be broken out of prison and returned to his rightful position atop of the throne I sit," she said.

"Okay, so that means that everyone is trying to do what it is that you want. You'll get him back, and this will all be over soon."

"It's not that simple, and you know that. You are thinking that the man that I want free is of a romantic love interest, but you are mistaken. He's my father. After you took my Viktor and Paco from me, my life's focus became revenge, and for that, I needed to amass power, which my father has always had. I never was a direct part of his business, but I wasn't ignorant of it either, so when I needed to learn, he was eager to teach me. By the time that he got caught up in Texas, I was more than capable and prepared to assume the position as his successor. Then good fortune smiled on me by putting Ty in my path. Soon, my father will be free, and my revenge will be had, but..."

She paused in speaking and just stared off into space, seeing something that was only meant for her.

"But what?" I asked.

"I'm not sure what happens after this mission is completed. I hadn't thought that far ahead, and there still isn't a real guarantee that the prison break can be pulled off. But for the first time, I'm confronted with the idea of what happens next. I'll have my dad back... and a new baby on the way, so that should be enough, right?"

The look in her eyes told me that there was something hidden, maybe even a secret desire that she hadn't fully acknowledged yet, but I didn't know what it was. As soon as I opened my mouth to ask her about that, I heard the sounds of footsteps running up the hallway toward us, and my mind focused on that. One of her men burst into the room, speaking so fast that even I had a hard time keeping up with him. The sweat on his forehead, and the scowl that was causing his face to fight itself, made it clear that whatever was going on was bad. Then, I caught the words 'shooting outside' fly from his mouth.

My first thought was of Ty, but then, I felt the hope inside of me swell because I knew that she wouldn't be attempting a bold ass rescue mission by herself. In my mind, I was seeing visions of my dad and my sisters shooting their way into this building with the blood of revenge in their eyes and determination radiating from their soul. I'd had no doubt that they'd come for me. The question had always been when and how. Now that the moment was upon me, I knew that I had to be prepared for the fight. Suddenly, Marta stopped spitting rapid fire Instructions, to which her man had been listening, and then he left the room without saying another word.

"Everything okay?" I asked innocently.

"I don't know yet, but don't worry because I'm prepared for anything," she replied, walking out of the room.

My stomach was sad to see the food go with her, but I comforted myself with thoughts of the feast that I would have once I was back in Russia. That would be my second order of business, right after I spent time reuniting with my wife and daughter. It felt like an eternity since I'd held Stormy, and I missed her in a fierce way. I would never consider any child that came from Marta and I as mine or any part of me, but Stormy was my daughter for life, and this situation had heightened that bond in my heart. I heard

Marta's familiar footsteps headed in my direction, but for once, I didn't feel the usual amount of dread that I normally would.

"This might hurt a little," she warned, coming back into the room, headed in my direction.

At first, I didn't know what she meant, but then, I caught sight of the long needle in her hand. Confusion immediately clouded my mind, and by the time the S.O.S. message translated into action mode, she'd jammed the needle into my shoulder. I couldn't see what was in the syringe, but whatever it was, she pumped that shit straight into me.

"What-What the fuck are you doing?" I asked, feeling pain surge through me.

"Relax, it won't kill you. I just needed you to remain calm because we've got an unexpected change of location."

"Ch-Change?" I asked, slurring the word like I'd just finished a fifth of cognac.

"Yeah, we gotta relocate because Ty got into a shootout with someone right in front of the building. I don't know what it's about, but I'm not taking any chances of someone trying to get you back ahead of schedule because we've still got work to do. I can tell by the way that your speech just changed, and the faraway look in your eyes, that my secret potion is working like magic. You'll be completely immobilized yet conscious of everything that is going on around you. Fun, right?"

My brain demanded my mouth to open and cuss this bitch out, but that order wasn't followed at all. I couldn't even twitch my lips or scowl. I could only blink, and even that action was as slow as Heinz ketchup being poured from the bottom of the bottle. The smirk on Marta's face as she moved around, unlocking me from the bed that had become my prison, was infuriating enough to have me wishing for a miracle. All I wanted was the use of my hands again because I would sure enough choke the life out of this bitch. God must've been busy helping others, or on a bathroom break, because I was little more than a dead fish at this point. The helplessness of it made me want to cry and kill in equal measure.

Once she had me free from the bed, she wiggled me back into my boxer briefs, and then, she tied a black bandana around my face to act as a blindfold. I heard her retreat from the room, but it was only seconds before she was back and instructing someone to pick me up and carry me. Everything in me wanted to fight back, but I was as violent as wet laundry without a clothesline right about now. I was scooped up with ease and tossed over a nigga's shoulder like a damsel in distress as I was carried out of the room. My sense of direction was all off because of the blindfold, but I was able to recognize the sounds of doors opening and closing, elevator dings, and I could smell the air the moment that we stepped outside. I was thinking that she was going to throw me in the trunk until I heard her give the order to put me in the back of the limo with her. Riding in style meant comfort, but it also meant that there would be no prying eyes to see me in this damn near catatonic state. I heard the car's engine come to life, but I didn't know when we were moving until she pulled the blindfold up a little bit.

"You still with me?" she asked, staring down into my face.

I projected all the hate I could into my eyes and stared at her unflinchingly, which only made her laugh out loud.

"My sweet Royal, one day you will understand why it had to be this way, and you might even thank me for preserving your bloodline."

The fact that she had my head nestled in her lap and she was stroking my face like I was a fucking pet poodle had my fury rising faster, and it was enough to put tears in my eyes. So, I closed them. There was no way that I would sleep, but I could do my best to ignore this crazy bitch in order to keep myself from going insane right now.

"Papi, don't be like that. I know that you want your legacy to live on, even if you die. It's what every man of your caliber wants," she said.

I didn't take the bait and open my eyes back up, but I definitely heard everything that she said and everything that was implied within her statement. It had been the optimistic side of me that had believed she'd let me live after she got what she wanted, but realistically, that never made sense. After what she'd seen and heard me do when it came to her, Viktor, and Paco, it wouldn't have been hard for her to imagine what I would do to her once I was from under her thumb. For that reason alone, killing me was her only option, but it still didn't answer the question of how to deal with my family. Unless, of course, she spun some wild tale about how we'd been fucking freely so that she could use her illegitimate kid as leverage in hopes that my family wanted a piece of me to hold on to. That idea was too crazy to work, but I wasn't about to bet my life on it, which meant that I needed to find a way to stay alive. I needed to use this move to my advantage in order to build some type of trust between her and I, so I focused my mind on ways to accomplish that.

We rode in silence for a while, and then, I heard her giving directions to one of her men about which plane to pull up beside. I opened my eyes in the hopes of glimpsing something useful, but she immediately lowered the blindfold back into place which sealed me in darkness. I heard the engine shut off and car doors open, and then, I smelled the fresh air again. A few minutes later, I heard the familiar roar of a plane's engine, followed by Marta giving instructions to get me on board so that I could get another shot. The fighter in me kicked in automatically, but I still couldn't bust a grape in a fruit fight, so it was all ass kicking in my mind. A few minutes later, the blindfold was lifted again, and Marta was staring down at me while holding up a syringe for me to look at.

"This is gonna knock you out for a while, but it won't kill you, and I'm not gonna steal your kidney," she said, smiling.

I blinked once so that she would know that I heard her, but I kept my emotions neutral. Immediately, I could tell that she noticed because she just stared at me for a moment, hesitating to put the needle in me for some reason. Instinct caused me to wink at her, which caused her to smile and blush in a genuine way that infused a hint of surprise into her expression. I closed my eyes, and a few moments later, I felt a wave hit me hard enough to make me feel like I was fighting a nineteen-year-old Iron Mike Tyson.

The last thing that I heard was Marta telling someone to load up and take off, and then, I was unconscious.

When I was younger, my mother liked to teach me things that would prove useful to me one day, and some of those lessons came from the book of *Metu Neter*. The importance of this book was unlocking the true knowledge of self that we all possessed, and the key to it was to look within. Through dream, meditation, or trance, one could find the jewels of new life that existed long before man came into this form. This book and those lessons were what awaited me in my unconscious state. When I saw my mother, I didn't feel the same anxiousness that had accompanied her presence before, but instead, her image symbolized hope. Unbeknownst to me, she had prepared me for all obstacles that life had to offer, only I didn't realize it until now. When my eyes finally opened again, I felt sluggish but more focused than I'd been in quite a while.

"I was almost worried that I gave you too much," Marta said.

I blinked a couple times and looked around the bedroom that we were in, immediately noticing that I could move my neck again.

"Was that a horse tranquilizer?" I asked, shaking my head slightly to clear my thoughts.

"Something like that. It actually turned into a stronger cocktail than I originally planned because you had to be given another sedative before the operation."

"Operation? What operation?" I asked, looking over at her from my prone position on the bed.

She smiled at me before pulling the top of her sundress down and showing me a bright red incision covered with fresh stitches right above her heart. I had no doubt that it was new because I'd seen every inch of her naked flesh on a consistent basis, but I didn't understand why I had to be sedated for her to have surgery.

"I don't understand," I said.

"We've got matching scars now."

When her words finally penetrated the ignorance of my brain, I looked down at my own chest and saw the exact same incision over my heart too.

"What the fuck did you do to me?" I asked, instantly struggling against the cuffs that had me restrained to the bed.

"Calm down. You should not exert yourself so soon after a major surgery. The doctor said that we must both take our time recovering over the next few days, which means that our love making will have to be slow and patient," she said, smiling mischievously.

"Marta, what the fuck did you do to me?" I asked with barely contained fury.

"It's simple. I gave us both a life insurance policy to make sure that we don't come to a premature end," she replied.

"What?"

The confusion on my face had to be obvious because I could damn sure feel it wrinkling my forehead.

"Listen to me closely, Royal. If my heart stops then so does yours, which means that we're joined together for life. Til death do us part."

Chapter 8

(David) (Two Days Later)

"How are you feeling?" Carrie asked, taking a seat beside me on the veranda.

"Physically, I'm fine, but everything else is up in the air. I never noticed how big this house was until Shaomi's huge personality wasn't filling it."

"I understand that. How is Dayjah taking the news?" she asked.

"She's been really quiet, and she spends most of her time with her brother, Prince David, watching over him like she's his new mom. It's cute, but I know that my baby is hurting."

"Of course she is. I mean, who wouldn't be after losing their mother at such a young age? All that we can really do is love her enough for her to feel safe," she said.

I nodded in understanding because the pain of losing my parents was still as strong as if it had just happened, instead of it being years ago. The loss of Tonya and our baby was just as fresh, and I still hadn't processed how I felt about losing the baby Shaomi had been pregnant with. I knew that Dayjah would never get over losing her mom, but she would get through it, and I would make sure that we did that together.

"She's been spending a lot of time with her cousins, which is helping her because she's never had such a big family surround her," I said.

"Family can mean everything to you if you're surrounded by the right ones, and from what I've seen, your people are filled with love and light."

"They definitely are, but they're also impatient, so what did you find out?" I asked, switching my train of thought toward the business.

"Well, your theory turned out to be a solid one because your uncle hasn't been seen anywhere in Ghana. I checked all the possible escapes that Tesha could've used. Apparently, she flew in with her team of hittas, and then, once they'd fucked shit up at your compound, they took your uncle and flew back out."

"Where did they go?" I asked.

"As far as I can tell, they went to Nigeria, which makes sense because Royal has a compound there, and he definitely has a loyal following."

"Those hittas ain't loyal to him. They're loyal to the money. I want you to throw out a price that will make a couple of them switch sides so that we can know exactly what to expect when we attack the compound," I said.

"Okay, and I, uh, looked into that other thing we talked about too."

When I looked over at her, I immediately saw the unease on her beautiful features, and I knew that I wasn't going to like what she had to say.

"Tell me," I demanded softly.

"Your name is not on any type of documentation when it comes to Stormy. It's only Tesha's and Royal's. He's listed as her father, and he signed the birth certificate, which entitles him to all the legal rights that a father has. To make matters worse, all of this took place in Russia where him and his family got juice like you and your family do over here."

"Which means that I have no legal recourse to make them hand my daughter over," I said, shaking my head in frustration.

"I'm sorry, David. I know that's not what you wanted to hear."

The last thing that any real father wanted to hear was that he was being kept away from his kid, especially when it was being done on some vindictive, petty ass shit. The shit that Tesha had done when it came to our daughter was done just to hurt me, but what she'd actually done was put our child in danger because the world thought that child belonged to Royal. The list of enemies that the Walkers had was way different than anybody who wanted smoke with me, and that was the path that Tesha's dumb ass had put our innocent daughter on. I wanted to kill her for that, but that was just one more reason in a long list of reasons. I pulled my phone out of the pocket of the silk robe that I was wearing, and I sent Ty a text with the info that Carrie had just passed along. It wasn't like I expected her to care the same way that I did when it came to Stormy, but if I wanted to rebuild trust, then I had to be honest on all fronts right now.

"Where exactly is Ty right now?" Carrie asked.

"She's still in Mexico, laying low in Sinaloa and waiting to find out what prison Felipe is in. She wanted to cross back into Texas since the cops already have Tesha booked on her capital murder charge, but I told her that would be a dumb move on her part."

"You still love her," Carrie said, smiling.

"What?"

"You damn well heard me, negro. I said that you're still fucked up about Tynesha, and it's obvious to anyone with eyes," she replied confidently.

"You're exaggerating, don't you think? I mean, yeah, we talked about our issues while I was in the hospital, but that's not saying that we're back together."

"Oh, I didn't say that you were back together. I simply said that you still love her. Look me in my eyes and tell me that I'm wrong, David."

I looked right over at her, intending to accept the challenge that she'd just thrown down, but suddenly, my mouth wouldn't work. The smirk that she gave me didn't help matters, but it did earn her the middle finger that I flipped her way. She laughed it off, and the knowledge that she was right never dissipated from her brown eyes.

"Okay, so what if you're right? I love you too, but that still don't affect where my life is right now," I said seriously.

The smirk instantly fell off of her face, and I could tell that she was as serious as a heart attack.

"You love me? What the fuck does that mean, David?"

"Why do you sound so surprised and... angry right now? Did you really think that you and I have gone through all that we have together and I didn't love your crazy ass?" I asked, confused by her response.

"What I thought was... Well, I don't know what the fuck I thought, but love definitely wasn't it."

"Okay, just tell me that you don't love me too," I said, smiling at her.

"That's not fair! You can't say some shit like that and then hit a bitch with the panty dropper smile."

"Whatever, just stop avoiding the question, Carrie."

"I'm not avoiding a muthafuckin thing, but I know that you're not ready to have this conversation with me, so just drop it," she replied, shaking her head.

I was more curious than ever now, but I could definitely see the warning lights flashing in her eyes, and that made me hesitate a little.

"I didn't know that you and I had secrets," I said.

"Of course we have secrets between us, you dummy! I'm married and basically living a whole double life at this point, but that was my choice because I knew exactly what I was doing when we started fucking. I just didn't think we'd get this far, and I didn't consider all the consequences."

"Meaning what?" I asked.

"Meaning that we would come to love each other, and..."

The ringing phone in my hand froze the rest of her statement, but I fully intended to finish this conversation at some point because she'd just admitted to loving me. Right now though, I turned my attention to my phone's screen as Ty's face popped into view.

"What's shakin?" I asked.

"I've got good news, bad news, and worse news," Ty said.

"I don't like my options but give me the bad news first," I replied.

"Okay, well, the bad news is that we're gonna absolutely need to work together with Royal's family in order to get Marta's dad out of prison."

"Okay what's the good news?" I asked, already trying to anticipate more shit after any good that could be uttered.

"The good news is that Royal's sisters are still being held in Mexico City. I reached out to his family so that I could relay Marta's demands and tell them that they had been detained for reasons beyond my knowledge. I let them think that Tesha was with me, which will give me time to pull up and get Stormy."

"Wait, what?!" I asked, knowing that I hadn't heard her crazy ass right.

"Before you freak out, I just want you to listen for a second. There's no way that these people can tell the difference between me and Tesha, especially because they've never seen us together. More importantly, there's no way that Royal's other sister or father is gonna take a kid with them to Mexico, and I know that they're headed to Mexico because I told them that we could link up and formulate a plan. That means that whoever is watching Stormy has an even less chance of knowing the difference between me and Tesha. I'm just taking a page from her playbook and doing it better."

"Ty, this is crazy though, and it could go all wrong. Why do it?" I asked.

"Because no matter how it happened, Stormy is here, and she's your child. I've cost you one child already so just let me make sure that your daughter is safe, okay?"

I was speechless. I could tell by the look in her eyes that she was being completely genuine, and the sacrifice that she was willing to make made me remember the woman that I'd fell in love with. It was truly amazing to see her returning to old form, and I knew that the best thing that I could do was let her do her.

"So, what's the worse news?" I asked, shifting in my seat.

"Well, from what I've been able to figure out, they're holding Felipe in one of two prisons. He's either in Colorado at ADX Florence, or he's in Guantanamo Bay."

"I thought Guantanamo was shut down," I said.

"Nope, that was a myth, but anyone who's there is just waiting to die basically."

"Isn't ADX that supermax that's underground somewhere in a mountain?" Carrie asked.

I nodded my head, understanding that this shit just went from hard to impossible.

"I don't think nobody has ever escaped from either one of those prisons," I said, feeling defeat and frustration in equal measure.

"That only means that we're about to make history, so don't even trip," Ty replied, giving me a wink.

"Your ass is just crazy enough to actually enjoy this shit, ain't you?" I asked.

Her laughter was enough of an answer, and it made me shake my head as I fought the smile that I could feel creeping across my face.

"I'll be there with Stormy as soon as I can. What are you and Carrie doing?" she asked.

The feeling of guilt that hit me was so sudden and foreign that I immediately went into a coughing fit, which caused me to double over in pain from the gunshot wound that I was still healing from.

"Are you okay?" Carrie asked, quickly moving to my side.

"Yeah, I'm good. Spit just went down the wrong tube," I replied.

I could hear Carrie snickering, but my focus was on Ty because my phone was still clutched in my grip.

"You good? If I didn't know any better, I'd think that my question made you nervous, which could only mean that your ass is up to something. Don't try to lie to me either because I'll smack you," she insisted.

I sat all the way back up on my chair, and I could see Carrie staring at me out of the corner of my eye, but I kept my focus on Tynesha. I'd vowed to give her honesty after our come to Jesus in the hospital, but even God would understand why now damn sure wasn't the time to expose this last secret love affair. The truth was no one's friend, least of all mine.

"Carrie and I were just talking about my Uncle Umar and the fact that Tesha is probably holding him at Royal's compound in Nigeria," I replied smoothly.

"Do you have intel to back that theory up?" Ty asked.

"Yeah," I replied.

She got quiet for a few seconds, but I could see the storm building behind her eyes, which usually signaled that she was cooking up something. I finally glanced over at Carrie and found her eyes locked on my face, but her expression remained neutral.

"Okay, I think that I should be able to pull the same trick on whatever guards are at Royal's place. Once I drop Stormy off at home, then I'll make that move to get Uncle Umar back," Ty said.

"Let's focus on one thing at a time, Ty. Don't start running around like your ass is bulletproof just because you share a face with your sister. It could be discovered any time that she's sitting in your place in that Texas jail cell," I warned.

"Yeah, I hear you. I'll call you once I've got your daughter, and I'll be safe. DON'T do anything stupid, David, and I mean that."

Before I could tell a lie, she hung up in my face, which was somewhat of a relief for real.

"So, are we going to Nigeria or what?" Carrie asked immediately.

"No, I've got another plan now."

I didn't elaborate. I just made a quick call to have the plane ready for us to takeoff as soon as possible.

"If we're not going to Nigeria, then just where in the hell are we going, David?"

"Our first stop is Texas, and then, we'll figure it out from there," I replied.

"And why the fuck would we go anywhere near Texas or the United States for that matter, especially considering the fact that you're still wanted?"

"Except that I'm NOT wanted, remember? Ty actually killing Roland paid that debt, so I'm free to move about the country, and I always wanted to have a thick Texas porterhouse steak from a real Texas roadhouse," I said, smiling.

"Don't get cute, negro, because it's not funny. Why are we going back for real?"

"Because Ty has the right idea by rounding up all of my kids. Getting them all in one location stops them from being the puppet strings that I'm pulled by because they are my ultimate vulnerability. Ty told me the name of the nurse that she gave our daughter to, so we're gonna track her down and get my baby back. After a little detour," I explained.

"Elaborate on what you mean by detour because that sounds real suspicious."

I tried simply giving her my most charming smile, but she didn't take the bait this time.

"Woman, you really don't like surprises, do you? Well, if you must know, we're gonna stop in and see Tesha and find out if she has anything useful to say. I'd say that it's a safe bet that she's feeling scared and alone, so that combination of vulnerable is something that can be exploited," I replied.

"Oh, wow. For a second, I almost felt bad for her with the way that you said all of that."

"I understand, Carrie, and I'd probably feel bad too if this wasn't a bed of her own making at this point. Tesha chose to make me her enemy, and that's crazy because I thought that we were so much better than that."

"I guess it is what it is because ain't no crying over spilled milk. You'd do well to remember that," she stated.

"What's that supposed to mean?"

"Oh, you'll see since you like secrets so much," she replied, chuckling.

Something about the look in her eyes gave me a chill, and I was actually turned on by the slight fear that she'd caused.

"Carrie, what are you not telling me?"

"Nothing that you haven't already heard before, but we'll talk about that when we make a little pit stop," she replied.

"A pit stop where exactly?"

"To our secret hideaway in good ole Georgia. You remember what happened in Georgia, don't you, David?"

Chapter 9

(Tynesha) (Russia)

The moment that I crossed over into Russian airspace, I felt nauseous, but I knew that it was just my nerves fucking with me. I kept my cool with great effort, even though I was sure that it looked easy to the people I was passing by. When I landed, I rented a Chevy SUV with a built-in car seat, and with David's help on tech support, I'd headed for the big ass castle that Royal and Tesha had been calling home. As I pulled up to the gate, I had a fleeting thought of how bad this could go if there was a password or secret handshake Tesha used to gain access to this massive estate. This notion was contemplated for all of five seconds before two guards with guns appeared out of nowhere and strategically surrounded the vehicle. I kept my cool and lowered the window enough for my face to be seen, while making sure to fix my expression so that it was one of expectancy.

"Good afternoon, Mrs. Walker, and welcome home. Your mother-in-law, Madeline, is up at the house with the children, and we're doing both exterior and interior perimeter checks every half an hour."

"Excellent. I will be leaving back out shortly," I replied.

He gave a curt nod and stepped away from the SUV so that I could continue to drive on through. From a distance, the castle had looked big, but as I got closer to it, the only word that came in mind to really describe it was colossal. I had no doubt that this structure was in somebody's history books because it undoubtedly belonged to someone with old Russian money, maybe an oligarch or a mobster.

When I came to a stop in front of the steps leading up to the huge front door, I cleared my mind of the frivolous thoughts and put my game face on. I hopped out and made my way to the door, where I almost fucked up and raised my hand to knock, like I was some type of guest or something. The options that I had quickly cycled through my mind, and the only thing that made sense was for me to act like I owned this muthafucka and everything in it. Given the intense security precautions, I had a hunch that the door was unlocked, and when I'd confirmed this, I walked straight in. Instinctively, I knew that I was about to get lost if I started running around, and that was sure to give away my identity. That meant that I needed to come up with a plan real quick.

I could smell food cooking, so I followed my nose in that direction until I came to a restaurant sized kitchen. There was a chef working some pots and pans like a DJ would the turntables, and his assistant seemed to be a cute white chick with brown hair. I hesitated before I called her mom because something inside me told me that no matter how close Tesha felt to this woman, she wouldn't call her mom.

"Madeline," I said.

Her head snapped in my direction immediately, and I saw relief flood her face as she came toward me.

"Oh, my God, Tesha, are you okay? Did they hurt you? Did they let all of you go?"

"I'm fine, and I don't know if they let Destiny and Angel go because nobody would tell me anything. When they let me go, I just ran and never looked back. I just wanted to get home to my daughter because I thought… I thought that I was never gonna see her again," I said, allowing real emotion to come through as I thought about my own missing daughter.

There wasn't a moment that passed when I didn't miss my little girl or her brother, and what made it worse was that

I couldn't even envision her face because I'd never seen it. My own daughter was a gorgeous ghost to me.

"I understand, sweetie, and I'm glad that you made it out alive. Free and Jonathan went to Mexico to try and get you all out, so if they didn't let Angel and Destiny go, then they will shortly. I'm expecting a call anytime now."

I felt my heartbeat quicken because I knew that the moment she received that call, there would be a whole lot more questions, and I had no good answers.

"Where's Stormy? I just wanna lose myself in her innocence for a little while," I said.

"She's right through there, in the first living room with the nanny and the rest of the kids. Go ahead and I'll call you when the food is done."

I instinctively hugged her for a brief second before turning and heading for the door she'd indicated. There were a handful of children stretched out on the floor, captivated by the eighty-inch flat screen TV on the wall playing cartoons. I spotted the nanny sitting on the couch, bouncing a baby on her lap, and even from the distance of across the room, I could see David all over Stormy's features. I had no idea how Tesha had planned to pass this little girl off as anyone's child besides my husband's because Stormy was literally David's mini me.

I walked straight over to the couch and held my arms out toward her. As soon as Stormy saw me, she squealed in delight, and I could feel the smile stretch across my face instantly while my heart beat like a jackhammer in my chest.

"Oh, Mrs. Walker, I didn't know that you were back. I was just about to make her a bottle," the nanny said, passing Stormy to me.

I was so caught up in the light and beauty of my niece/stepdaughter that I ignored the nanny and turned to walk away from her without a second glance. The sound of Stormy's gibberish reminded me of her brother, Rashon, and my heart hurt because my baby wasn't with me. All I could do was hug Stormy close and will myself to hold my emotions together as my mind tried to think through my exit strategy. When I walked back into the kitchen, Madeline was busy with the chef, which made the job of grabbing a bottle from the refrigerator and heating it up easier. The last thing that I needed was for Stormy to get hungry and act a damn fool while I was trying to sneak her out of here. Once the bottle was ready, I took it and headed back out of the kitchen toward the front door. I kept waiting to hear Madeline's or someone else's voice tell me to halt and hand over the baby, but that didn't happen, and within a few minutes, I had Stormy strapped into the car seat.

"Okay, sweetie, let's go meet your daddy and the rest of your family," I said, propping the bottle up in front of her so that she could eat.

Once that was done, I got behind the wheel and pulled off. Thankfully, this time, I didn't even have to stop at the gate. It was simply opened for me, and I was allowed to cruise right on through. As soon as I made it off of the property, I stopped and took a picture of Stormy, which I immediately sent to David so that he would know I'd succeeded. No sooner had I pulled off again, he messaged me, thanking me and saying that he owed me for this. The thoughts of how he could repay me made me smile, but I shifted my focus to the next leg of this journey. It took me half an hour to get to the airport, and by that time, I was terrified that an Amber Alert would've already been broadcast with my picture attached to it. I didn't meet any resistance as I drove back onto the tarmac and headed for the plane that I'd rented, and five minutes later, I was sitting in the plush, leather chair with Stormy in my lap, dozing off. When we started to taxi for takeoff, I breathed my first sigh of relief, even though I knew that I still had at least one more miracle to pull off. I spent the flight to Ghana formulating a plan while watching Stormy sleep peacefully in my arms, and by the time we touched down, I felt confident in what I had to do. I summoned the army, as was my power as their queen, and I didn't leave the plane until General Udoku arrived with his men.

"General, I have good intel that General Umar is in Nigeria, being held at a compound there. We will go retrieve him immediately."

"With all due respect, my queen, I must insist that you remain in the safety of your own compound and let us handle the mission of recovering the general," Udoku replied.

"I understand your position, but Umar is family, and I will not sit by while he suffers. Plus, this rescue mission will turn into a blood bath without me because the compound where Umar is being held belongs to my twin sister and her husband. Because both of them are indisposed at the moment, I will simply be allowed to walk in and demand Umar's release without question or confrontation. I've already discussed this plan with the king ,and we are in agreement. What I need from you and your men is an escort, just in case shit should go wrong, and I need someone to take the princess back to the compound."

He nodded once and then issued instructions to his men. Even though it had been my idea, it still wasn't easy to hand Stormy over, and I had a sneaky suspicion that my feelings were triggered by the memory of giving my own daughter up. I did now what I had to do then, and I handed her off in order to keep her safe. It took another fifteen minutes for General Udoku and eight of his men to load up their weapons, and then, it was time to go back amongst the clouds that were changing colors with the sky.

By the time we landed in Nigeria, it was pitch black, and the feeling that gave me was ominous, but I brushed it off. Once I got a Sprinter van rented, we loaded up and headed out. The ride was quiet besides the sounds of weapons being loaded, but I knew that everyone was extremely focused on the task that lay ahead. I was of the mind frame that this would be as easy as when I'd picked up Stormy, but the overall tension of this war ready group of men had me wanting to reach for my own pistol. When I pulled up to the gate, I took a deep breath and put my game face back on. Four men emerged from the shadows, clutching AKs aimed at the van, but I felt no panic because I reasoned that their actions were due to a foreign vehicle pulling up on private property. I lowered the window and stuck my head out.

"Open the gate. I'm in a hurry," I said impatiently.

"Sorry, Mrs. Walker," a man said, stepping back and waving another man out of the way.

Once they moved, I sped through and drove straight to the house I saw in the distance.

"Stay in the van," I said, hopping out and waiting for the guards to approach me.

A group of five men eventually showed up out of the darkness, and that signaled the curtain going up on act two of this play.

"Listen up. A deal has been made, and we've agreed to release General Umar, so I need him brought to me immediately," I said.

I'd expected quick movements to my instructions, but not one man moved. They all just stood there, staring at me like I was naked and peeling a banana real slow for their entertainment.

"I'm speaking English, and I know that you understand, so what is the hold up?" I asked, voicing my irritation.

They looked back and forth between each other, and then, one brave soul stepped forward.

"M-Ma'am, we have a problem, and we tried to notify Mr. Walker, but..."

"What's the problem? My husband is dealing with something important, and he's unavailable, so whatever the issue is, you can tell me," I said, feeling that ominous feeling return with force.

"The, uh, the general tried to escape, and he was shot."

"Okay, I assume that you got him medical care, so where is he?" I asked.

"He-He was shot in the head. There was no need for medical care."

My eyes closed involuntarily, and I could feel my heart shift as tears built inside me from the well of sorrow.

"You're saying that he's dead?" I asked, still not opening my eyes in a defiant attempt to deny the truth.

"Yes, ma'am, he's dead."

"Where's his body?" I asked.

The silence that followed this question caused me to finally open my eyes to look at each man individually. The secret delight I saw in their eyes stoked the fires of my pain until it became anger.

"I asked you a question," I said, taking a threatening step toward the group.

"We burned it."

"You-You what?" I asked in a low growl.

I heard the sound of the van door easing open, but the men in front of me were completely focused on me and not the threat that they couldn't see.

"We burned it, trapping his soul so that he could not cross to the ancestral plan," he replied.

I opened my mouth to berate the man with every foul word that I could think of, but before I could, bullets started flying past my head, dropping the man who had been speaking. Before I realized it, my gun was out, and I was firing randomly at the men in front of me. I hit two in the face before bullets started coming back at me, forcing me to stop, drop, and roll like my house was on fire. Udoku's men immediately hopped out and joined the fire fight, which effectively put the odds in our favor and laid the opps to rest. There was no time to celebrate or feel relief because, suddenly, lights came on all around the compound, and that only meant one thing.

"We gotta go," I said, getting up and running toward the van.

"No, we fight!" Udoku declared, swiftly changing the clip in his gun for a full one.

His men followed his lead, which left me with a decision to make. A queen couldn't be timid or afraid, or she would lose the faith of her people. She couldn't be foolish either though because other lives hung in the balance as well. Fight or flight. I dropped the clip from my gun into my hand and counted the bullets, quickly realizing that I didn't have enough dogs for this fight. I popped the clip back in, tucked my pistol, and ran toward the fallen men a few feet away to scoop up an AK-47 and any extra clips off of the dead bodies. I could hear men yelling in an African dialect that I didn't understand, but the tone was clear.

As soon as I spotted movement coming from the house, I raised the AK and let that bitch speak with a pronounced stutter. The chorus of bullets coming from Udoku's men was a sweet harmony that encouraged me to stay on the offensive and move toward the house. None of us knew how many men were on the premises, so it was prudent to think in terms of worst case scenarios and assume that we were heavily outgunned.

"What's the plan, General?!" I yelled over the constant gunshots.

"Kill everyone you see," he replied.

"We're outnumbered, so it's gonna be kinda hard to kill them all. We need a better plan than that," I insisted, still firing steadily at the shadows trying to close in.

He didn't respond; he just kept shooting, and that was definitely not the confidence booster that me and his men needed in this situation.

"You can be on a suicide mission on your own time, but you won't take any of us with you. I want everybody back in the van NOW!" I yelled, reversing course and retreating while still shooting.

I got no argument or push back from Udoku or his men, and a few moments later, we were back in the safety of the Sprinter van with me behind the wheel.

"Hang on," I said, quickly starting the engine and standing on the gas pedal with all my weight.

I pulled a one hundred eighty degree turn as fast as I could, and we caught half a dozen bullets broadside, but that didn't faze me in the slightest. The first thought that popped into my head was that I definitely wasn't getting the deposit back that I'd put down on the van, and I laughed out loud.

"What could possibly be funny?" Udoku asked in a bewildered tone.

"You wouldn't understand. Just hold on," I instructed, aiming for the wrought iron gate in front of us while keeping my foot on the gas.

Since I wasn't getting my money back anyway, I was going to drive this bitch like I stole it and save our lives in the process.

Chapter 10

(Tesha) (Texas)

"I want my fucking phone call!" I screamed, kicking the metal door to my cell to demonstrate my displeasure.

I'd been trying to play nice and keep shit cute since I'd been dragged from Mexico across the border to my current location, but enough was a goddamn enough!

"Ayo! I want my muthafuckin..."

"Bitch, shut up because don't nobody care what the fuck you want!"

I spun around with the quickness, staring daggers at the big tittie Mexican bitch I'd been forced to share the cell with. We hadn't exchanged but a few words, but I could tell from the jump that she was the bullying type who thought that she could run everything and everyone. We were about the same height, and she outweighed me by like fifty pounds without counting the twenty-pound bowling balls for titties on her chest. I was way prettier though, and I knew that was part of the reason that she thought that she could whoop me.

"I advise you to mind your damn business," I said, locking eyes with her.

She rolled off of her back and stood up, smiling at me in a way that telegraphed darkness with ill intentions.

"I can make you my business if that's what you want."

I didn't need to hear anymore words, nor give any, because it was obvious how this shit was about to go down. Without hesitation, I closed the distance between us in one step, bringing a swift right jab with me that landed squarely in between her lips. She flew backwards onto the bed, but I was on her ass before she could gather her thoughts about what had just happened. I rode her chest like a sports bra, sending a combination of left and right jabs at her face until fresh blood covered her from chin to forehead like wet paint. It was plain to see that she was dazed and quickly approaching the land of unconscious, but that didn't make me let up on the gas in the slightest. With my left hand wrapped around her windpipe, I fired precise, methodical right jabs to her nose until I heard it crunch loudly like a beer can. This made her holler, and it made me smile. I hopped off of her long enough to pull her by the legs off of the bunk, and then, I stomped her muthafuckin ass in the face until she was unconscious with blood pooling under her head. The physical exertion of the beat down I'd just issued felt amazing, almost as good as sex, but I still wasn't completely satisfied, so I returned to the door and continued banging. After a couple of minutes, I heard the sound of keys headed in my direction, and I paused to see if the person attached to them was headed for me.

"If you keep making all that damn noise down here, you'll be going into a nice, padded room on a psych hold," a tall, white lady cop threatened.

"I want my phone call," I demanded.

"Yeah, well, I want my husband to have a bigger dick, and I want my dude on the side to divorce his wife so that his big dick is all mine. Neither of those things is likely to happen, so my suggestion is that you shut the fuck up and deal with it like I have to do."

"It's my right to make a phone call. You can't just lock me up and not let me call my lawyer or my family and not let me see a judge. This ain't the goddamn 1800s!" I replied, feeling the strong desire to choke this bitch come over me.

"In case you haven't been told, I'll go ahead and enlighten you. You are currently being detained on a federal hold by the U.S. Marshals, and even though you're technically here, you're still a ghost in our system. Once that hold is lifted, you'll be allowed all the freedoms that the great state of Texas has to offer, including the death penalty. Now, is there anything else I can help you with?"

Her condescending tone was making the hairs on the back of my neck stand up, and I was now wondering if her bravery would remain intact when this door was no longer between us. There was only one way to find out.

"I don't need your help, but my cellmate could use some medical attention," I replied, stepping away from the door so that the cop could see inside the cell.

"Oh, shit."

"No, that's blood, not shit, and I suggest that you get somebody down here before this bitch bleeds out," I said, smiling.

"This is Officer Parker. 1033! I need medical attention down here to booking ASAP. Cell 241," she said frantically into her two-way radio.

A squawking reply came back, but I didn't understand it because I wasn't close enough to catch the words spoken. All I knew for sure was that they were coming.

"Bishop, step back and face the wall. NOW."

"How many times do I gotta tell you dumb ass people that I'm NOT Tynesha Bishop. I'm her twin sister, Tesha Walker," I replied with swiftly building anger.

"I don't give a fuck who you are. I just know that if you don't step back and let us in to help her, then you're gonna have another murder charge on your hands."

As badly as I wanted to be defiant, I knew that I had to think this shit through. Eventually, I'd be able to prove that I wasn't my sister, but if this bitch did die, then it wouldn't make a bit of difference who I was in this 'hang em high' state of Texas. I backed up and faced the wall just as rapidly approaching footsteps reached my ears.

"Don't move," Parker instructed.

I heard the key turn in the lock, and a few seconds later, I was handcuffed and damn near yanked off my feet.

"Put her in a single cell and somebody get a camera so that we can get pictures," she instructed.

I was roughly pulled from the cell by two big, burly, white guys who looked like they pushed tractors around for entertainment on the weekends.

"Either of you muthafuckas harms me in any way, you'll have to answer to my husband," I warned.

"Shut the fuck up," one of them said.

They carried me between them around a corner, stopping in front of a door that was open. While one of them took the cuffs off, the other one held me still by grabbing a fistful of my hair and wrapping it around his hand until my roots were tight against his knuckles. I wanted to move instinctively, but losing a patch of hair would have been that bullshit that made me fight to the death.

"Is that T. Bishop?" a male voice asked from behind me.

"Yes, sir."

"Bring her back out because her lawyers here," he instructed.

The one handcuff that had been removed was quickly put back on, and I was spun around where I came face to face with a tall, muscular built, Black man wearing lieutenant bars.

His name tag said *Boone*, and his face didn't look at all friendly, so I kept my smartass mouth shut. I knew damn well that I hadn't called a lawyer. Royal was still being held for ransom, and two of my sisters-in-law were somewhere in the Mexican justice system. So, that only left the rest of my in-laws in Russia, but it was entirely possible that they had orchestrated this with the various contacts they had in the States. Either way, I wasn't about to do or say anything impulsive that could prevent me from seeing my lawyer right now.

"Let's go," Boone said, turning and walking away.

I was pushed in the back to prod forward movement, and I followed him down the hall through booking until we got to a door that sat back off in the cut.

"The cuffs stay on," Boone said, opening the door and stepping aside.

When I walked in the room, the first person I saw was Carrie sitting all prim and proper behind a long, gray, metal table. She had on a black pants suit, her hair was pulled into a functional ponytail, and she was looking basic enough to be an unassuming white girl. Movement caught in my peripheral vision had my head moving to the right, and suddenly, I couldn't breathe because there stood David in a blue pinstripe suit, looking professionally deadly. My steps faltered, and I pulled up short. I wanted to turn around and retrace my steps, but I heard the door shut behind me with the finality of a coffin lid closing.

"Have a seat, Tynesha," David said.

"Nigga, you know that's not my name," I replied in a low growl.

"Easy, Tynesha. We're here to help," Carrie said, smirking.

"My husband is gonna kill both of you," I vowed, shaking my head in frustration that their deaths couldn't happen right now.

"Yeah, well, that's tomorrow's problem so sit down and let's talk," he said.

"We don't got shit to talk about, nigga."

"Are you sure? Because I thought that you might wanna talk about Stormy," he replied calmly.

This time, it was me who smirked because this nigga was delusional if he thought that he could leverage this legal misunderstanding into getting my daughter.

"Talk about Stormy for what? There's no reason to talk about *my* daughter."

"T, what the fuck happened to you? When did you become this heartless ass bitch who would keep a child away from their father?" Carrie asked, looking at me with genuine concern.

For a second, my mind went blank, and not even a smartass reply popped up. Introspection took over, and I actually found myself wondering when and why the war between me and David had started. The instant pain that I felt from that question made me shut the door on those answers though, and I retreated into the safety of my animosity.

"My child's father is Royal. That's the daddy that she knows, and that's the one that she'll continue to know, so if that's all you came to talk about, then you wasted your time," I said.

"Okay, how bout we come back to that? Why don't you explain why you were in Mexico City getting into a shootout?" David said.

"Because that bitch shot at me first!"

"Given what you did in Africa, and making everyone think that it was her, can you really blame her? I mean, you put a target on her back that got her shot," Carrie said.

"Well, obviously the bitch ain't die, and am I supposed to feel bad? She was the one who said that she was gonna kill me and my baby!" I replied defensively.

"Again, can you blame her? I mean, damn, T, you fucked her husband and got pregnant by the nigga. I know that it was an accident, and none of us meant for anything like that to happen, but good dick has its consequences," Carrie stated.

"Spoken like someone who knows," I replied, staring at her differently now.

She kept a straight face, but I could feel David's energy shift, and that told me everything that I needed to know.

"Shaomi is dead, and that shit is partially on you. Now, you can continue this war amongst us, or we can focus on getting your husband back and keeping our daughter safe," David said.

"What do you know about Royal?" I asked.

"That he's being held by a woman who's demanding that we break her father out of prison and that Royal sacrifice his child," David replied.

Some of this info was known to me, but the part about sacrificing a child was definitely new to me. There was no way that I was sacrificing my child or my husband.

"I'm not about to agree to no shit like that," I declared.

"I feel the same way, and that's why we're working on a plan, but in order for that shit to work, we've gotta play nice. That includes you with your sister too," David said, looking pointedly at me.

"What sister?" I asked, smirking.

The frustration on David's face gave me a feeling of pleasure that was very much needed given the current legal entanglement I was caught up in.

"Come on, Tesha. You're smarter than this. Fuck all the petty bullshit because it's bigger than that at this point, and I know that you can see that shit. Leave the past in the past," Carrie pleaded, looking at me with such an earnest look that I wanted to gag.

"Look, I don't need to play nice with you two, Tynesha, or anybody else for that matter. Me and my real family will help bring Royal home, and we will keep Stormy safe. You all can do whatever the fuck you wanna do," I said.

"It's not that fucking simple, Tesha, because that same bitch who has Royal has me and Ty's son too! She's holding my son hostage until she gets what she wants, which means that whether you like it or not, we're in this shit together," David stated angrily, moving until he was standing right in front of me.

I could tell by the pain in his eyes that he was telling me the absolute truth, and for a split second, I let my guard down and felt that anguish with him.

"H-How did she get your son?" I asked.

"By not giving Ty a choice and Royal only made it worse when he showed up looking for Ty," he replied.

The instant guilt that I felt came from the knowledge that Royal's moves had been guided by my desires. On some level, I'd set this in motion by not being able to let go of the issues I had with Ty, David, and Shaomi. That knowledge caused a physical ache in my chest, and it took everything inside me to fight that pain and guilt in order to keep my emotional detachment in place.

"Look, I'm sorry to hear that, but I've gotta worry about me and mine," I said.

"Don't you get it, you silly bitch? There's no way around working together, so get your fucking mind used to the idea or be prepared to lose it all," Carrie said angrily.

"I'm not bout to lose a goddamn thing except for my patience if either of you keep trying to convince me to play nice. We ain't family, and we ain't friends, so you both can miss me with all this sappy ass, hand holding type shit," I said.

For a while, they both just stared at me and said nothing, and then, David shook his head while reaching inside his inside suit pocket.

"You know, on the way here, I kept telling Carrie that you weren't gonna be reasonable, no matter how nice we asked or how much sense we made. It's like that nigga, Royal, started dicking you down, and you lost all your muthafuckin common sense or something. I should probably feel a little insulted, or at least have some wounded pride, but I guess that I don't because of the consolation prize that I get instead."

"Oh, yeah, and what's that? Her?" I asked, nodding toward Carrie with a smirk on my face.

"Nah, my consolation prize is that I'm smarter than you, and I know which side to pick in this war," he replied, smiling as he pulled his phone out and started scrolling through it.

"Smarter than me, huh? And yet, here you are, begging for my help like a weak nigga would," I replied, chuckling softly.

He laughed along with me, and then, he turned his phone so that I could see the screen. The laughter got stuck in my throat, and the smile died on my face instantly as the reality of what I was seeing registered in my heart.

"That's-That's Stormy. That's my baby. How did you get that picture?" I asked weakly.

"Your sister took it when she picked Stormy up from your castle in Russia," he whispered, smiling from ear to ear.

"David-David, what are you doing? Why would you and Ty do that?" I asked, trying to catch my breath.

"Because she's my daughter, not Royal's, and I'll be the one to keep her safe. You can sit your dumb ass in here and think about that."

Chapter 11

(Royal)

My hand went to my chest out of reflex to scratch the annoying ass itch of the scar that was still trying to heal, but all I got for my efforts were the plastic zip ties biting harder into my flesh. This being strapped down to a bed shit was getting old to me, and I'd bided my time long enough.

"Marta!" I yelled, feeling my anger in the increase of my heart rate and the sweat on my brow. I could feel the patience surrounding that anger like my mother's loving arms, and I embraced it to the point that I was opening my mouth to let some ugly shit fly, but she walked into the room first.

"What do you want, Royal? I was on an important business call."

"I want you to unstrap me from this muthafuckin bed and let me move around," I demanded.

I expected an instant refusal, but I could tell by the look in her eyes that she was entertaining something as a result of what I'd said. Ordinarily, I would've waited her out to hear her decision, but today wasn't that day.

"Did you hear what the fuck I said? Because you're not moving," I stated.

"Oh, I heard you, and I'm trying to figure out a compromise."

"Woman, damn a compromise! Just stop the bullshit and let me up from this bed," I replied angrily.

The smirk that appeared on her face was cute and annoying all at the same damn time, and it really made me want to shoot the shit out of her.

"I know that you are a smart man, Royal, and for that reason, I know that you understand the necessity of compromise in any relationship, no matter how dysfunctional that relationship is. So, we can find that compromise, or I can go back to the business I was handling."

On a good day, I hated ultimatums, and I tended to do the opposite, just to be spiteful, but this wasn't that type of day, so I knew that I had to do something different. I didn't like it though.

"Compromise how?" I asked begrudgingly.

"I'll show you," she replied, turning and leaving the room.

When she came back a few moments later, she had more zip ties in her hands, along with a box cutter. Trailing her was one of her henchmen carrying his trusty AK-47. She cut my hands free first before cuffing them individually, and then, she secured them together with another zip tie in the middle. Once those were secure, she did the same thing to my ankles, and then, she took a step back to admire her handiwork.

"We good?" I asked, sitting up and swinging my legs to the floor.

"Almost, we just need one final test."

The way that she said it sounded normal, but I could see the malice in her eyes as she held out her hand to her hired gun. He placed some type of collar in her palm, and she held it up for me to see.

"The fuck you think you're about to do with that?" I asked, already gearing up my mind to fight.

"Well, the way I see it, you've got two choices. I can put it around your neck as I intended, or I can wrap it around that pretty dick of yours. 50,000 volts is gonna hurt a lot more when it blazes a path straight through your most prized possession, but that's just my thoughts on it. What do you think?"

It was on the tip of my tongue to tell this sick, twisted bitch exactly what I thought, but the thought of my family allowed me to maintain my cool.

"50,000 volts, huh? Well, that might just stop my heart either way, and you know exactly where that leaves you, don't you, sweetheart?" I asked sarcastically.

"Oh, I thought about that exact same thing, which is why I talked to the doctor, just to make sure we were good. I was told that it would hurt like a motherfucker, and you would probably lose control of your bowels, but you'll definitely live through the experience. Unless I get a little too carried away," she replied, smiling in a way that only the devil himself could appreciate.

I didn't know if she was lying, but I did know that the bitch was suicidal for damn sure, which made her the last person I wanted to play chicken with.

"If I were you, I wouldn't wrap it around my dick because it might make your ride uncomfortable," I said.

"Touché, salesman," she replied, moving toward me with the collar outstretched in her hands. This was, by far, the most humiliating thing I'd endured in my life, but it reminded me of a quote I'd read in a book once. *Expect no mercy from the hands of those that you betray.* Deep down, I knew that Marta hated me, and the fact that she was cumming on my dick regularly would never change that. The child that she was trying to create wouldn't be created out of love. It was being made from a hatred so strong and deep that it had consumed this woman's soul. I didn't know who she'd been before that fateful night when I'd killed her son, but she was absolutely the red devil in every sense of the word now, and I felt responsible in a way.

"If you try to leave the property, you'll get a taste of those 50,000 until you're back inside the perimeter. Do it at your own risk," she advised, fastening the collar around my neck until it clicked metallically.

"I'll be a good dog."

"Oh, that will make for interesting role play at some point, but as always, there must be some business before pleasure. I'm going to shoot a short video of you to send to your family because I need to make sure that proof of life was actually given to them," she said, taking a few steps back and pulling out her phone.

"What's wrong, Marta, you don't trust your messenger girl?"

"I trust no one except the dead because I know exactly what they're gonna do. I haven't heard from Tynesha since the day that she left from my penthouses, so I don't know if that shooting did her in or what, but either way, I need to make sure that the show goes on. Now, look at the camera and speak clearly," she directed, holding her phone up.

I did as she instructed while trying to put together the right words in my mind before opening my mouth. There was so much that I felt like I needed to say, but I knew that this was yet another test by Marta and one that surely had dire consequences. The only play that I had was to continue to play shit smart and wait on my moment. When Marta pointed at me, I took a deep breath and spoke the first thing that popped into my mind.

"I am Royal Walker, son of FatherGod, husband to a queen, and the brother of the most powerful forces in the world. I don't know where I am, but I want all of you to know that I'm okay. I stand on bidness, and I expect the rest of you to do the same."

I didn't say another word, but I was looking past the phone being held to the woman who was actually holding it because my message was for her too. After a few seconds of silence, she lowered the phone, and then, her focus was locked in on her screen as she did whatever she felt was necessary before sending it. When she was done, her phone disappeared into the pocket of her form fitting cargo pants as she signaled her man to leave, and her attention returned to me as she came slowly toward me.

"There is a darkness inside you, Royal, and it's incredibly sexy to me. I don't know where it comes from, but I would wager that it comes from some incredible pain and torment before this time in your life," she said.

"I don't know what you're talking about."

"That's a lie, and we both know it. The night that you killed my Paco, I was too blinded by anguish to see it, but I've been watching you since you stepped into my building, and I know that you know the beast that lives within you. I dare say that you actually control him, and that's probably the sexiest part of all to me because you're still so young. Our child will truly be something amazing," she said, taking a hold of my dick through my boxer briefs.

The passion inside her blazed up at me from her smoldering eyes and entwined with it was the insanity that I'd come to expect. The detest that I felt wasn't for the sexual act that she was initiating with her slow massage of my dick. It was the truth of the words that she'd spoken about my darkness. I knew that I was different, and I'd known that for a long time now, but I hated that this person could see so clearly what I'd worked so hard to hide. She knew too much, and that gave her the advantage for the moment. I was starting to see how I could turn the tide though. I took a step backwards, away from her, which removed her hand from my now hard dick. Without taking my eyes off of hers, I slowly pushed my boxer briefs down over my hips a little until my dick sprang free like a Jack in the Box that was pointed at her. She fought the urge to look down at it, but the twitch in her cheek was a dead giveaway.

"What are you waiting for?" I asked.

"What do you mean?"

"I'm mean that this dick won't suck itself... so get on your knees and show me how good that pretty mouth is," I demanded.

For a brief moment, utter shock took a hold of her features, but she recovered quickly, and then, all I saw was her unapologetic desire that literally brought her to her knees. With her left hand, she guided my dick into her open mouth, and she used her lips to slowly suck me to the back of her warm throat. The feeling could only be described as putting a sweater on a snake, and it took every ounce of my willpower to keep a straight face full of detachment. Her eyes never left mine, and I saw the sheer determination in her to succeed in domination, but she didn't understand that I was tapped into my own darkness. That meant that she wouldn't beat me, and I wouldn't submit. Her technique went from curious and tentative to deep throating perfection in a matter of seconds, and I knew instantly that this was definitely going to be a battle. I let her have a few moments of thinking that she could break me this easy, and then, I smirked down at her. The heat and hate that filled her eyes could be felt in the saliva in her mouth, but I didn't focus on that because I knew that I needed my full concentration now. Her speed changed, and her lack of gag reflex had my dick hammering the back of her throat like a carpenter with a nail gun. I blinked long and slow, but I knew that she could still see the steel of my spine remaining gun barrel straight. The involuntary tears leaking from the corner of her eyes gave me a sick feeling of pleasure that only made my dick harder, and I knew that she could feel it in her jaws. Still, I refused to give in, and she refused to give up. We were ten minutes in when she grabbed me by my ass cheeks and caught a rhythm that had me fucking her face without me having to move for real. The flush of her face told me that she was putting that work in, which sent a tingle up my spine.

"Stop," I demanded.

She complied, but my dick stayed locked in between her lips and jaws as she stared up at me with an odd mix of obedience and defiance all in one.

"Get up against the wall," I told her.

With reluctance, she released me from her mouth and positioned herself against the nearest wall. I shuffled awkwardly until I was standing a few inches behind her.

"Pants and panties at your ankles, Marta."

"I'm not wearing panties," she replied breathlessly as she quickly pushed her pants down.

I took the last step forward to put me right up against her, causing her to widen her stance in welcome. With my hands still bound, it was difficult to maneuver, but once I got the head of my dick inside her, I raised my arms and wrapped them around her neck. With the plastic zip tie pressed right up against her throat, I was able to lace my fingers behind her head, slightly choking her, and that was when I rammed my dick up inside her. The force of my stroke pushed her up on her tiptoes, which made her gag and moan at the same time.

"R-Royal," she croaked.

"Shhh, just take it. This is what you wanted, remember?" I whispered, fucking her steadily with long strokes.

"Mmm hmm."

This wasn't about us making love. This was all about hate and darkness, and I gave myself over to it. I fucked her without mercy, alternating between light choking and completely severing her air supply until I felt her body's panic cause her pussy to clench me in a Vulcan death grip. When she came, it felt like she would never stop, and only then did I give her what she wanted. As my cum filled her up, I was choking her with enough force to lift her off of her feet, and my powerful strokes kept her pinned to the wall in front of us like a fly on a windshield. My vision clouded over, so intense was my orgasm, and I lost my balance, which caused us both to fall to the floor. She pulled my arms from around her neck, and I could hear her sucking in huge gulps of air, but she didn't try to move off of me. We laid there for a while until she eventually rolled over and crawled to her feet, and then, she helped me up.

"I-I don't know what the fuck that was, but I have NEVER experienced that before. I could feel how much you hated me with each and every throb of your dick inside me, and I swear that it only turned me on more," she admitted, fixing her clothing.

I didn't say shit. I simply pulled my underwear back up and sat on the bed, staring at her with a blank expression. My lack of response caused her to look at me long and hard, and then, she reached into her pocket and pulled out her box cutter. No words were spoken as she bent down and cut both my legs and my hands free.

"Are you hungry?" she asked, turning and walking from the room.

I took my time following her out, while trying to quiet the round of applause my mind was giving me for a job well done. There was no sense in getting cocky because I still had an electronic leash around my neck, not to mention the booby trap on my heart. I may not have been restrained, but I was a long way from freedom. It wasn't until I stepped into the living room that I realized just how far away I was. The open floor plan that allowed me to glimpse the living room, dining room, and kitchen made the log cabin seem huge, and the clouds outside of the balcony window made me feel like I was in heaven. I knew better though because this wasn't heaven. It was hell, and every moment was an eternity spent.

"Where are we?" I asked.

"What do you want to eat? I'll cook you whatever you have a taste for. All you gotta do is tell me what you want."

"I wanna know where we're at," I said again.

"It's not important where we are. All that's important is the goals that have been set and their achievement."

I walked casually down the three steps that led to the living room and kept moving until I got to the balcony door. As soon as I pulled the door open and took a step outside, the collar around my neck started beeping in warning, and I could literally feel it powering up.

"I wouldn't go any farther, Royal, or you'll be shocked with what you learn."

My fury mounted quickly, causing me to turn around and advance on her like a leopard when its prey was cornered. She didn't flinch, not even when my hand went around her throat, and I backed her into the refrigerator forcefully. I heard her breath rush out of her lungs, but the sound of the gun cocking beside me was louder.

"Jefa, you want me to shoot him?"

"No, it's okay. He won't hurt me," she replied.

"You willing to bet your life on that?" I asked.

"Yep, are you?" she asked.

"Marta, stop fucking playing with me and tell me where the fuck we are," I growled through clenched teeth.

"If you must know, we're at one of my vacation spots. We're in Geneva, Switzerland. Feel better now?" she asked, smiling.

I didn't feel better. I felt like I'd reached the end of the earth. I felt like I was all alone.

Chapter 12

(David)

The sounds of Tesha banging on the metal door, screaming for me to come back, rang in my ears all the way out of the police station and back to the car.

"What happened to her? Why does she hate us so much?" Carrie asked, climbing into the passenger seat.

I slid behind the wheel of the Mustang and started the engine as I contemplated the answer. I'd been asking myself the same question, but it wasn't until I'd actually been face to face with her that I realized how completely off her whole attitude toward us was.

"To be real with you, Carrie, I don't think that it's hate driving her. I think that it's fear and pain, but the only way that she knows how to deal with it and maintain her sanity is through intense anger."

"Well, that definitely sounds like some psychobabble bullshit," she replied, shaking her head.

"That don't make it less true," I said, putting the car in gear and driving off.

"Okay, well, true or not doesn't matter because at the end of the day, her funky ass attitude ain't helping nobody. That shit is gonna get people killed, including her darling husband, but this bitch acts like she don't understand none of that."

"You're right, but me having Stormy definitely got her attention, and now, she has something to think about while she sits on the sidelines. My focus is on my kids right now," I said.

"All of them?"

"Of course that means all of them. What type of question is that?" I asked, glancing over at her.

"Never mind. Forget it. Where are we headed now?"

We came to a red light when she asked that question, which allowed me to look at her with my full attention because I felt like she had something to say.

"Why are you staring at me like that?" she asked.

"Because if you got something to say, I'mma need you to say it with your chest."

"Nah, I'm good. I just need to know what we doing next because I'm hungry, and a bitch got jet lag," she replied, rubbing her face.

"We can grab something to eat and catch a few hours of sleep. Can you book us a room real quick?"

She nodded and pulled out her phone, and I began looking for the nearest fast-food place to make a pit stop at. My choices were between pizza and burgers, so I chose to pull up at Domino's and run inside to place our order. While I waited on the pizza, hot wings, and brownie desserts, I pulled my own phone out to call Ty and check in with her. When she didn't answer, I felt some slight worry and a little déjà vu, but I didn't panic. My next call was to my staff at the house in Ghana, and I was told that Ty had been there to drop my daughter, Stormy, off before leaving again. This information put things into perspective because it meant that more than likely, Ty was on to her next mission of rescuing my Uncle Umar. I wouldn't keep calling her because I wanted her to focus on the dangerous task at hand. I spoke with Dayjah for a little while, explaining to her that Stormy was her little sister and that she needed to protect her like she did Prince David. The pensive expression on her face was adorable, but it paled in comparison to the big smile that she gave me before she promised to take care of her siblings.

When I was alerted that our food was ready, I got off of the phone, collected my order, and headed back to the car.

"Where are we headed?" I asked, passing Carrie the food and sliding back behind the wheel.

"Just follow the GPS and we should be there in no time."

I did as instructed, and fifteen minutes later, we pulled up at a ranch that, from the looks of things, had been converted into hotel bungalows spread out across a few acres.

"Cozy," I said, nodding approvingly.

"Privacy was the goal just in case we end up doing something that is gonna bring police attention."

"Good thinking because you know how you get," I replied, chuckling, climbing out of the car.

I went around to the passenger side and opened the door so that I could take the food back and let her get out of the car.

"They already sent the key card to my phone so let me swipe it at the door and let you in before I grab the bags," she said, moving around me and heading for bungalow number eight. I followed her inside, headed for the spacious living room instead of the kitchen that was positioned toward the back. The interior design was done in a Western theme with a rustic feel, but it was easy to see that all of the amenities were modern and top of the line. This was definitely a weekend getaway spot where couples turned off their phones and really got into each other in every sense of the word. For the briefest moment, my mind went rogue in a naughty way, but I shook the images away and set the food down. By the time I'd retrieved the paper plates from the kitchen, Carrie was coming back through the door with both of our duffel bags, one in each hand.

"Did you know that the kitchen is fully stocked?" I asked.

"Yeah, that's part of the exclusive services offered. They don't call it 'a little slice of Heaven' for nothing."

"This was definitely a great choice on your part. My only question is what do you want to drink with your food?" I asked.

"Beer goes great with pizza so bring me something cold and smooth. I'm going to change."

"I got you," I replied, returning to the kitchen and grabbing two beers.

I saw her disappear with our bags into the one bedroom, so I decided to go ahead and make us plates of food. By the time she came back into the living room, I had a hot wing on the way to my mouth, but her presence made me pause real quick.

"Is that my T-shirt you're wearing?" I asked, looking closely at the Baltimore Ravens T-shirt that hung on her body seductively.

"Yeah, it is. Thanks for fixing my plate," she said, sitting down beside me.

My shirt was naturally big on her, but somehow, it still managed to hug her curves in a way that was sexy as fuck. I had to swallow twice before I was finally able to sink my teeth into the piece of chicken in my hand. I really wasn't tasting shit though because I was eating with my eyes, and she was the feast.

"So, uh, why are you wearing my shirt exactly?"

"Because it's comfortable, and I didn't bring anything appropriate to sleep in. I mean, unless you would prefer that I slept naked beside you," she said, looking at me with a devious smile.

The chicken in my mouth naturally picked that moment to head down the wrong tube in my throat, causing me to choke and cough hard enough to immediately have me drop the chicken and pick up my beer. Her laughter was melodic and rich, and the twinkle in her eyes was dangerous enough to telegraph her intentions fairly clearly for our brief stay in this secluded hideout.

"So, we're spending the night?" I asked.

"Well, yeah. This ain't exactly a spot that you rent by the hour, plus I know that you gotta be feeling that jet lag by now, so you need to rest. It makes logical sense to hole up here and get a fresh start tomorrow... Or the day after."

I laughed out loud at the innocent look that she had fixed on her face while shaking my head.

"Why do I feel like you're trying to seduce me?" I asked.

My question was ignored by her as she grabbed her a slice of pepperoni pizza and became preoccupied with eating in earnest. I let it slide for the moment and went back to eating myself.

"You wanna watch the game?" she asked, grabbing the remote and pointing it at the sixty-five-inch flat screen hanging from the wall.

"Basketball or football?"

"Well, basketball is my preference, but I'll let you be great if you wanna watch football," she replied.

"Don't talk shit to me while you're wearing the greatest football team alive on your back right now, thank you very much. And for your info, I love basketball more, so find a Lakers game and hush."

"The Lakers? What you know bout the SHOWTIME Lakers?" she asked, looking over at me somewhat surprised.

"Girl, please. If you're a Lakers fan, then you're probably a Lebron James Lakers fan."

"Negro, you keep forgetting that I'm older than you, so don't let the flawless skin fool you. And for your information, I'm a Magic Johnson Lakers fan, even though he insists that Kobe Bryant was the greatest Laker of all time," she replied in a matter-of-fact tone.

"Okay, my bad, pardon, pardon," I said, using a fake British accent while putting my hands up in surrender and laughing.

"Yeah, I thought so."

Her arrogance made her even more sexy, which created a question in my mind that needed answering. After putting my beer down, I reached out and put my hand on hers, forcing her to lower the remote and look at me.

"Why are you acting like you and I ain't never kicked it?" I asked.

"And by kicked it, you mean..."

"Been alone together, chilled together, had incredible sex. You can take your pick of whatever definition fits right now," I replied.

"I mean, you're right, and we've done all of the above, but that seems like so long ago, David. We barely spoke to each other over the last year, and now, you think that we can just fall back into old habits like we never missed a day? That's realistic to you?"

I thought about what she was saying for a brief moment before I gently pulled on her hand to bring her closer to me.

"Yeah, that's realistic to me because we have chemistry. That's all we need," I whispered, putting my hand on the back of her neck and pulling her mouth to mine.

She didn't resist, and I kissed her passionately until I could feel the strength of her heartbeat thumping in her smudge proof lipstick. Instead of pulling back, she surrendered to the moment and immediately climbed into my lap. When I put my hands underneath the T-shirt that she had on, I quickly realized that she was naked, and I was grateful for the lack of obstacles between me and fulfillment. I could tell that she felt the same way because she was so preoccupied with getting my zipper down and my dick out that she wouldn't even raise her arms so that I could peel the shirt off of her. As soon as she had my dick out, she lifted up and took me inside her tight, hot pussy without hesitation. She was already so wet that I could feel her juices racing down my shaft faster than she could ride to the bottom, but I wasn't complaining.

"Go slow," I mumbled.

"Shut up," she replied before taking my bottom lip in between her teeth and biting down.

Her bite had just the right amount of pressure to mix pleasure and pain, but it was the immediate gallop that she jumped into that threatened my sanity. Within seconds, I was balls deep inside her, and her pussy juices were building faster than a category four hurricane spinning off the Florida coast. The fact that she still had my lip in between her teeth made it impossible for me to utter a plea, threat, or warning, which left my only option as one of submission to the moment. My hands slid around her thick ass cheeks, and I grabbed her hard enough to leave my fingerprints forever in her delicate flesh. In that position of pushing and pulling, we fucked like two teenagers trying not to get caught, and we both came with ugly sounding threats in under five minutes flat. When she finally let go of my lip, I could taste blood in my mouth, but I honestly didn't give a damn because the only thing that was on my mind was making her tap the fuck out in round two. I didn't say shit. I simply stood up with her still in my arms and my dick still buried inside her.

"Wh-What are you doing?" she asked breathlessly, kissing my neck.

"Evening the score," I replied, carrying her across the living room into the bedroom.

When I turned on the lights, I saw the comfortable looking king-sized bed a few steps away, and I headed straight for it. I laid her down gently before stepping back to take my clothes off, and then, my attention was back on her as I finally pulled the T-shirt off her.

"Are you ready to go again?" she asked, smiling seductively.

"Shut up," I demanded.

With a plan of action in my mind, I started kissing her neck on her left side and worked my way to the right side while using my tongue as the perfect segue way. My ears were tuned into her body like she was embodying my favorite love song, and I listened intently while working my way downward. Feather light kisses across her titties stopped her breathing altogether, and when I used my tongue to run laps around her nipples, her back arched involuntarily.

"Fuck, David, what are you doing to me?" she moaned, grabbing my hair.

My response came in the form of sucking and licking until she was whimpering with need. Lower still I moved, kissing down her stomach with one destination in mind, but the sight of a horizontal scar froze me.

"Wh-Why did you stop? D-David, why did you stop?"

"This scar right here… I don't remember it being here before," I said slowly.

Her whole body tensed up instantly, and it would've been impossible for me not to recognize that the mood had definitely shifted. She didn't utter a word though, and when I leaned back to look up at her, the look of fright on her face was as real as the orgasm had been.

"Carrie..."

She shook her head from side to side, but her eyes stayed locked on mine.

"Don't do this, David."

"Where did you get this scar?" I asked, ignoring her plea.

"David, don't."

I could see the tears filling the spaces where so much passion had dwelled a short time ago, and that was all the conformation I needed.

I climbed onto the bed beside her and pulled her into my arms. The moment that her head hit my chest, I felt her tears falling, and that kept me quiet for a minute while I decided how best to deal with this situation.

"You know that I meant it when I told you that I love you, right?" I asked.

"I know, but... that's not always enough."

"In this case, love is all we need, so tell me the truth," I insisted.

"T-Tell you what?"

"Tell me about the baby that you had sometime in the past year because I know that scar is from a C-section birth. Is the baby mine or your husband's?"

"My husband and I are separated," she said softly.

"That's not what I asked you."

In her silence, I could feel her gathering her strength, but in my heart, I knew what the answer was because her earlier comments were now flooding my mind.

"Carrie?"

"You don't need me to say it, David, because you already know. The baby that I had was yours."

Chapter 13

(Tynesha)

The run for freedom that we'd made on the crazy drive back to the plane was done with my adrenaline on full tilt, and that kinetic energy in my body didn't dissipate once we were airborne. Throughout the entire flight, my mind was struggling between grief and trying to find the words to tell David what happened. I knew how much he loved and respected his uncle, so I knew that the pain of this loss would be unbearable no matter what pretty words I conjured up in my mind. Umar meant a lot to me too, and not just because he'd married David and I but because of how close we'd become in the days after David had gotten shot in Florida. Almost losing David had been devastating for both of us, but we'd shared in the pain so that it couldn't drown us both. The gentle spirit that Umar had, mixed with just the right amount of fire and madness, made him a man to be loved if he was on your team. He was a general of the people, but in a short period of time, he'd become family to me in a fatherly way, and that was what was making my heart heavy.

When we landed in Ghana, I instructed Udoku to go back to the house and guard it with his life in case any type of attack was launched in retaliation. He assured me that the lockdown protocol would be implemented immediately, and then, him and his soldiers left me alone. I gave instructions for the plane to be refueled for a quick turnaround, even though I was undecided about my next move or destination.

There was no way that I could tell David about his uncle over the phone because I could still see the fury in his eyes when he'd thought that my only crime had been kidnapping Umar. Knowing that his uncle was dead would plunge him into a world of darkness and having that happen while he was off doing something dangerous could get him killed. I didn't know exactly what him and Carrie were up to, but I knew that it came with an element of danger just because of how our lives were setup right now.

After pulling out my phone, I sent him a text message, asking him where he was, and then, I turned my mind to what I could do next that was productive. It took half an hour for the plane to refuel, and by then, David still hadn't texted me back, so I was still confused about my next move. When the pilot came out of the cockpit and asked where we were going, I replied with the first thing that popped into my mind.

"Colorado. Get me to the closest city or town to the supermax prison, ADX Florence," I said.

He nodded curtly before turning and retreating back the way that he'd come. As we prepared to taxi, I refocused on my phone and started scanning through any and all info that I could find out about the prison and its architectural design. I poured over articles. and even some Colorado legislation involving the types of criminals sent to ADX Florence, until my eyes burned, and I was forced to give them a rest. It hasn't been my intention to fall asleep, but when my adrenaline finally subsided, I was knocked out in the comfortable leather chair. I didn't stir awake until the pilot announced our descent and imminent landing. When I lifted my phone off of my chest, I saw that David still hadn't texted me back, so I sent him another message repeating the question, and then, I ordered a car with a driver from the airport's exclusive car service. By the time we landed and stopped outside of the hangar, there was a royal blue Maybach with a slender brunette female standing beside it, waiting on me.

"Good morning, Queen Bishop. Right this way," she said, opening the back door for me.

I climbed in and waited for her to walk around and get in.

"Take me to the best hotel around," I instructed once she was seated behind the wheel.

"Yes, ma'am. That would be the local lodge and ski resort up the mountain."

"That's fine. What's the name of it?" I asked.

"Luxury Lodge."

I quickly pulled up the resort through a travel website and read about the amenities offered. The only thing that I was really worried about was privacy, so I made sure to rent three rooms that were all in a row, which allowed me to stay in the middle suite with no neighbors. I didn't know how long I'd be here doing reconnaissance work, but I ordered a couple weather appropriate outfits from the luxury gift shop and had them delivered to my room. My next move was to google search all lawyers within a fifty-mile radius because this would be my best source of information when it came to knowledge out here. By the time the car came to a stop in front of the lodge forty-five minutes later, I had the workings of a plan in full swing, and I was ready for action. I had about two hours to kill before my appointment with attorney Samuel King, which gave me enough time to freshen up and get something to eat.

"Do you live far from here?" I asked.

"About an hour away."

"Well, I'm not gonna ask you to go that far and then have to turn back around to come pick me up. I'll just get you a room here. What's your name?" I asked.

"My name is Felecia and thank you very much for being so considerate, ma'am."

"It's nothing and stop calling me ma'am because it makes me feel old as fuck. Just call me Q and keep it cute. Got me?"

"I gotchu," she replied, laughing.

"Good. Are you hungry because you can join me if you want to?"

"Oh, okay. Uh, that would be great," she said, obviously surprised by the invite.

Based on her looks, I could tell that she was maybe a year or two older than me, and she was local, which meant that she knew about the dirt under the fingernails of the people out here. If she proved to be useful, then that would make my task easier, but if not, it would only cost me a couple dollars.

"I'll wait for you inside while you park the car," I said, opening the door and stepping out into the brisk early morning air.

I walked up the stone steps to the lodge door and pulled it open to feel the warmth of heat accompanied by the smell of sweet hot chocolate. There was no need to bother with the front desk because my key card was on my phone already, so my attention turned to the restaurant on my left. As I approached it, I saw a hostess wearing a sexy, white dress with open toed, white sandals that showed off her sexy toes painted passion purple. Her nails matched, and the overall exotic Indian beauty made it all irrelevant.

"Do you have a reservation?" she asked in a soft, melodic voice.

My eyes scanned her chest, looking for her name tag, but there was none visible.

"No reservation, but I need a table for two unless you're free to join us," I replied, smiling enticingly.

The way that she blushed only enhanced her sex appeal, but I liked the way that she played it cool.

"Sounds interesting, and under different circumstances, it would be possible, but I'm on the clock right now. Follow me to your table."

My smile didn't falter as I fell into step behind her while my eyes scanned the cozy atmosphere that I was being led into. There was a roaring fire blazing to my left, classical music could be heard leaking from hidden speakers, and the conversations that I passed seemed both joyous and carefree. Despite the white dress of the hostess, the dress code of everyone in attendance seemed to be casual, but the fact that I had on shorts definitely made me stick out. I could care less though, and I took my seat with as much entitlement as everyone else around me.

"A waiter will be along shortly to take your order. Are you expecting your guest to arrive soon?" she asked.

I looked up in time to see Felecia weaving through the crowd, headed in our direction.

"She's right there."

When her eyes followed mine, I heard the sharp intake of breath.

"What are you doing here, Felecia?"

"The same thing that you are, Sarah. I'm working," Felecia replied, taking the seat opposite me.

"Do I even wanna know how you two know each other?" I asked, smirking.

"It's a long story," Felecia replied.

"Obviously not long enough. I'll send the waiter over," Sarah said, walking away from the table.

"I don't know what that was about, but I probably shouldn't have suggested a threesome a few moments ago," I said, chuckling.

The way that Felecia's mouth dropped open made me laugh out loud, which only added a fiery blush to her pale cheeks.

"If you're gonna run with me, you've gotta loosen up, Felecia. Besides, you gotta admit that my light skin beauty, mixed with your girlish sex appeal, and her native earthiness would make a combination that any man or woman would die to sample."

"I-I know. I mean, I agree. I'm just not used to a woman being so forward about her sexuality, especially with a complete stranger," she replied.

"I make no apologies."

"Oh, I wasn't looking for any type of apology, but my granddaddy raised me to be suspicious, so I'm looking for your motive," she replied candidly.

Her reaction made me laugh again and appreciate her obvious intellect.

"Your granddaddy sounds wise, so I won't insult either of your intelligence by saying that I want nothing more than to ride your face. I want information as well."

"What kind of information?" she asked warily.

"About this town, the people, and how all of that factors into the supermax prison that's hidden in one of these beautiful mountains."

"What's your interest in the prison?" she asked, cocking her head to the side.

The arrival of the waiter gave me time to formulate my pitch in my mind before I opened my mouth to try and sell it to her. We both ordered steaks, medium rare, with fries on the side, and two bottles of the house best mimosas.

"My interest is in the personal running of it, their shift changes, emergency protocols, and exactly what prisoners are being housed there," I said softly enough that none of the other patrons could overhear.

Her face became a mask of no expression, but her eyes radiated a clear understanding.

"Beautiful and crazy is a deadly combination. As my granddaddy would say, that's like rolling a cigarette made of gunpowder and using a stick or dynamite to light it."

"Obviously bad for your health, huh?" I asked, staring intently at her.

"Bad enough to fuck with my life expectancy and I'm not ready to do that at this ripe old age of twenty-five."

"I can understand that, but I'm not asking for you to get any more involved than the info I'm asking for, and I'll pay you well for that," I vowed.

"How much we talking?"

"If your info is good enough, then I'm open to negotiate any price that you think is fair," I replied.

"50k, nonnegotiable," she said, leaning across the table with her hand out.

I almost laughed in her face at the number she spit out just because it was lower than I imagined, but instead, I chose to use this as an opportunity to walk my talk.

"What's your account info?"

She pulled her phone out and unlocked it.

"Let's sync up and I'll transfer it to you," she replied.

I unlocked my phone and set it to allow for reception of her info, and then, I reached across the table. She tapped her phone to mine, and instantly, her account information popped up. It took me less than five minutes to transfer $150,000 from one of David's accounts to hers, and as soon as her phone pinged, I saw her eyes get huge.

"I said-I said $50,000," she stammered.

"I know what you said, but now you know how serious I am about getting what I want. Let's enjoy our meal for now though and we'll discuss business afterwards."

"After we eat or after you cum on my face?" she asked, grinning in a nice, naughty way.

I laughed as I raised my glass and took a healthy swig. She followed my lead, and then, we settled into a lighthearted conversation. Oddly enough, our interaction started to feel like a first date, but it wasn't awkward because we were able to just vibe and talk about whatever. Her company was refreshing and completely different from any experience that I could remember having with a female. Initially, I'd been bluffing about us fucking, but by the time we finished eating, I had to admit that my bi-curiousity was out in full force.

"Can I get you anything else?" the waiter asked.

"No, but you can charge the meal to room 2502 and give yourself a 15% tip on the bill," I replied.

"Very well, ma'am. Your room card please?" he requested, typing and then holding out his handheld electronic billing machine.

I quickly scrolled through my phone and unlocked my room card long enough to sync it to his device, and then, I reactivated the security protocol to prevent unauthorized expenditures.

"You two enjoy your day," he said as he left.

We sat there, staring at each other in silent, sensual communication with eye contact that was so direct and intense that it felt like we were touching.

"That was a great meal," I said.

"Yeah, it was, but... I could still eat more."

Her meaning was so clear that I felt my face go flame hot, and suddenly, I was playing defense instead of offense.

"Is this your first time?" she asked suddenly.

I instantly avoided the question by reaching for my glass and draining my mimosa in one gulp.

"Question made you thirsty, huh? It's okay. I'll be gentle with you," she said, holding her hands out to me.

I paused for a few minutes, and then, I placed my hand in hers as we both stood up. We walked from the restaurant hand in hand, which caused a heated glare from Sarah, but we both ignored it and proceeded to the elevator. The closer that we got to my room, the more nervous I felt, which translated into butterflies flapping around the food that I'd just ingested. By the time we actually got behind closed doors, I was ready to admit that I was going to need more liquor in my system before anything popped off .

"You want a drink?" I asked, letting her hand go and moving toward the full-size bar in the corner.

"Sure, I'll drink whatever you've got."

I giggled uncontrollably, and I could feel my face turning red again.

My phone started ringing in my hand before I could make a smartass reply, but when I saw David's face pop up, I was instantly reminded of tragedy.

"Hey, bae, what's up?" I asked as nonchalantly as I could.

"A lot is up, but we need to discuss it all face to face. I need you on the next thing smoking out of Africa, and I need you to come to Florida."

"Florida? Why the fuck am I coming back to Florida?" I asked, completely confused.

"Because that's where I am, and we need you here."

Before I could ask him who "we" consisted of, he'd turned his phone, and the face that popped up was one of a stranger yet completely familiar to my heart.

"That's-That's our daughter," I said, putting my hand to my mouth to conceal the sob trying to escape me.

"Her name is Rashawna," he replied.

"I still don't understand though, David. Why would you take her to Florida of all places? It's not safe there," I stated, feeling panicky.

"I know, but I had no choice. I'll explain when you get here so hurry up. And watch your back."

Chapter 14

(Tesha)

My hands were bloody and raw, but I couldn't feel the pain in them anymore. My blood on the metal door of the cell seemed to be mocking me in this moment, but I was too tired to resume the one-on-one fight we'd been having. Ever since David had knocked my world off of its axis by taunting me with the fact that he had my child, all I could see was red. All I could taste was rage and hatred infused with bitterness on my tongue, and it was choking me because I felt like I couldn't breathe. I'd been racking my brain for hours on end, but I was no closer to finding a solution on how to get the fuck out of jail than I was on how to get my baby back. Beating a bitch up and beating the door down hadn't gotten me so much as a phone call, so it was painfully obvious that I had to try something different. I just hadn't figured out what that different thing was. As far as the police knew, I had been afforded my rights because I'd had a meeting with my "attorneys" and trying to explain the truth would've been a waste of time. All I could do was wait now, and that was what I'd been doing despite how helpless and powerless it made me feel. The sound of a key turning in a lock drew my thoughts away from being trapped in my mind and caused me to question what fresh hell was coming next. The slot in my door for trays dropped open, and the face of a white woman wearing nurses' scrubs popped into view.

"Ms. Bishop?"

Everything in me wanted to scream at this skinny bitch about that not being my name, but a sudden idea popped into my mind.

"Yeah?" I replied, getting off of the bed and walking toward the door.

"The officer out here wanted me to check you for injuries."

I held up my hands so that she could see how fucked up they were, and by the gasp that I heard come from her, it was clear that she got the point.

"O-okay, just give me a few seconds," she said, disappearing from view.

I heard brief talking in the hallway, and then, one of the cops from earlier stepped back in front of my door.

"Put your hands out the slot in front of you and get cuffed," he demanded.

It was clear by his tone that he wasn't happy about whatever the nurse was making him do, but I didn't rub that in his face by being defiant. I did just as I was instructed, and a few moments later, I was being led up the hallway with the cop on one side of me and the nurse on the other side. I was taken to the medical department so that my bruised and bloody hands could be tended to, but I was hoping to take care of much more than that.

"What's your name?" I asked the nurse.

"Tasha."

I looked to the door to make sure the cop standing just outside of it wasn't eavesdropping.

"Look, Tasha, I'mma level wit you. I absolutely beat up that bitch I was in the cell with, and she deserved it, but my name isn't Tynesha Bishop. My name is Tesha, and I'm Ty's twin sister. I know that sounds farfetched as fuck and hard to believe, but all you have to do is run my DNA against hers and verify our existence with the hospital that we were born in back in Orlando, Florida. I know that it's not your job to do any of this, but I'm begging you. These cops don't give a fuck who I am because one of theirs is dead, and somebody has to pay the price for that. If you don't help, it'll be me paying that price, and I don't owe this debt," I said, staring at her with a pleading look on my face.

When I'd started talking, she'd paused in her work, and now, she resumed the cleanup of my hands even though she said nothing to my proposition. I desperately wanted to push the issue, but my instincts told me to be cool and bite my tongue because she was going to take the bait. It took a few minutes to clean and bandage my hands, and she still hadn't said another word, but I'd noticed how she'd discreetly set aside some of the bloody bandaging. She gave furtive glances toward the door before she hopped up off of the stool that she'd been sitting on and grabbed what looked like a long Q-Tip.

"Open your mouth," she whispered, working quickly.

I complied, and she swabbed my mouth. I could feel tears in my eyes because of the hope bubbling up in my chest, but I held them back and silently prayed that this was going to work.

"Stay out or trouble. If what you're saying is true, then this will all be worked out, but if you catch a charge out here, they're gonna push for the max penalty just because you're her sister," she warned.

I nodded my understanding and mouthed the words 'thank you,' and then, I prepared to press my luck by making another request.

"I need one more thing, Tasha, please. I need you to let my family know that I'm here because no one knows. The last thing that anyone heard was that I was in Mexico, and then, the Feds dragged me back across the border within hours of my arrest. My family is rich and powerful, and they will compensate you."

She was shaking her head like she wasn't even entertaining what I was proposing, but I saw the blue in her eyes light up when the word rich came out of my mouth.

Money made the world go round, and this chick was smart enough to know that.

"You gotta hurry up because it's almost count time," the cop called from the door.

"We're just about done," Tasha replied.

"All you gotta do is go on social media and look for any of the Walker sisters, Freedom, Angel, or Destiny. Tell them where I am and that I promised you $50,000 to relay this message. They'll send it without hesitation," I whispered.

Without turning around, I could feel the cop come into the room, but my eyes stayed locked on the nurse's face until she finally gave me a subtle nod. I felt the air rush out of me in a giant WHOOSH from the breath that I hadn't realized I'd been holding, but I played it off by standing up and moving toward the cop.

"What time do they feed us around here?" I asked.

"Shut up and let's go," he grumbled, grabbing the handcuffs and pulling me toward him.

He quickly checked to make sure that they were still locked, and then, he led me away from the room like a horse away from the troth.

"You ain't gotta drag me like this. It ain't like I'm gonna run no damn where," I said with growing frustration.

He ignored me completely and kept right on pulling me down the hallway like a scolded child. Everything in me wanted to kick his muthafuckin ass in the nuts, but I knew that the punishment for such a thing would be deadly at best. I kept my mouth shut, kept walking, and kept my mind focused on just surviving the next few hours until my crazy ass in-laws came through. My first order of business would be to kill David's bitch ass for having the nerve to play with my child. It didn't matter that he had contributed to her biologically because I was the one who'd carried her and cared for her while he was off fucking God knows who. I didn't feel any remorse for keeping Stormy away from David because, in truth, she had a better family and more stability in her environment with me and Royal. She was a Walker now, and they knew how to give her the love and loyalty that David could only pay lip service to because that nigga only loved himself. Being that he'd gone through the trouble or kidnapping Stormy, I knew now that the only way to stop him was to make him a permanent fixture on the ground. That would only be half of the problem resolved though. Without a doubt, I knew that I had to kill Tynesha, if for no other reason than the fact that she'd played in my family's face by taking my daughter. It didn't matter that David had put her up to the bullshit because, ultimately, this was her doing. Everything that had happened all came from her decision to fuck Roland because that was literally the paradigm shift that had forever changed everyone's life. That bitch's pussy was kryptonite, and I would love nothing more than to carve her uterus out with a spoon while she was still alive to feel it. The thought made me smile until I realized that I wasn't being led back to the cell that I'd been pulled out of to go see the nurse.

"Wh-Where are you taking me?" I asked.

My question was ignored, and he just kept pulling me behind him like I was a little red wagon or some shit. I'd seen enough movies and prison shows to know the horror stories about shit that happened to vulnerable females in this position, so the fear that I felt was instant and justified. I planted my feet in the ground with force and stopped walking, which caused him to pull up short and glare at me with eyes full of hatred.

"I asked you where are you..."

I didn't get to finish repeating the question before the back of his hand shot out like a viper and smacked me to the ground. Before I could even begin to scramble off my back to my feet, I felt his boot fly into my stomach with enough force to lift me off the ground, causing me to spit up the hot bile that rocketed up through my windpipes. Playing offense wasn't any type of option or possibility, which only left defense to keep me alive.

I was forced to curl into a ball in anticipation of more kicks, but they didn't come.

"Get your ass the fuck up!" he growled, grabbing me by the hair and yanking hard.

I wanted to resist, but it was either get up or lose a huge chunk of hair, so I allowed him to pull me to my feet. As soon as I got my feet planted, I felt him grab me by the handcuffs again, but instead of pulling me behind him again, he held on tightly to them and smacked me again with a vicious backhand. I could taste my blood in my mouth and the dirt from his hand, but my only focus was on remaining conscious.

"Okay, Okay!" I hollered, trying to raise my hands and ward off the next blow.

"That's what I thought," he said, pulling me by the cuffs hard enough to make me stumble and have to catch my balance.

He led me back past booking and farther down another hall, stopping when we came to another cell that was bigger than the last one. Not by much though. First, he unlocked the door to the cell, then he took the cuffs off of me and pushed me inside the darkened room. The lights flickered on just as the sound of the door closing behind me registered to my mind.

"Have fun," the cop said, laughing as he walked away.

I didn't turn around to watch him go. I just kept my eyes on the three Spanish bitches in front of me. None of them were taller than 5'4", but they all weighed at least two hundred pounds, and they were covered in ink that undoubtedly came from doing a prison bid somewhere.

"So, you're the bitch who beat up Priscilla?" one girl asked.

"I don't know. I guess. I didn't ask her name before I beat the blood out of her muthafuckin ass," I replied, showing no fear.

They were standing in a semicircle toward the back of the cell, and the look of mental instability in each woman's eyes made the cell seem smaller than I'd originally thought.

"Priscilla is our home girl. She's part of the Mexican Mafia, and we're untouchable," another girl announced.

"Apparently you can get touched if you fuck with the right bitch, and somebody should've told Priscilla that," I replied, still unfazed.

The three of them shared a look, and then, one of them began to advance on me slowly. My mind quickly assimilated a battle plan as I squared up with my hands in front of me and waited to damage this hoe's face. The decision was already made on my end that as soon as this bitch stepped within firing range, I was going to try to break everything my fist came into contact with. But right before she got close enough, the scene changed. My focus was on the woman in front of me, but all or a sudden, a blur of movement sent the signal to my brain for what was about to happen. Me being naïve had allowed me to assume that this was going to be a fair fight, but they were all moving at once. Even though I mentally adjusted and calculated quickly, I still only had enough time to throw two punches at the first target before I felt myself being pushed backwards into the door. As soon as my back hit the unyielding steel, I bounced back with forward momentum and ran smack into a right hook from one bitch that slid me into the left uppercut of another bitch. My knees buckled, but somebody's hands going around my throat stopped me from collapsing to the floor. That gift quickly turned into a curse because it became open season on my face, and punches came flying like bullets in a warzone. One of my eyes shut instantly right before the bones in my nose shattered, and my blood started gushing everywhere. I opened my mouth to scream that I had

AIDS, in hopes that all the blood flying would make these bitches back up, but before I said anything, I felt two of my teeth get punched to the back of my throat. I gagged but didn't get the chance to choke because a well-placed power punch to my temple took all the fight out of me and almost knocked me the fuck out. My brain was telling my hands and arms to move and fight back, but in my soul, I knew that I had no win coming.

"S-Stop," I mumbled, almost completely dazed and knowing that I had enough.

"Nah, we just getting started, bitch."

The next thing that I felt was several body blows that hurt bad enough to make me shit and piss on myself, but then they dropped me to the floor. I expected their feet to coming raining down on me next, but instead, all three of them surprised me by slowly backing up until they were back in their original positions across the room. I breathed a sigh of relief, and that sent a searing pain through my chest that made me cough hard enough to loosen my bowels again. The taste of blood had been in my mouth for so long that I was used to it, but when I coughed a bloody bubble, I began to panic. It was then that I realized that I hadn't been hit with body shots. I'd been stabbed repeatedly, and there was blood in my lungs.

"H-Help!" I cried out, reaching toward my attackers like they would suddenly become my saviors. Even in my weakened state, I could recognize their looks of joy, and their laughter was the last thing that I heard before the light went out.

Chapter 15

(Royal)

My mind tried to make sense of her words, but none of what she'd said seemed real. How the hell was her relocation spot Geneva, Switzerland? I didn't know NOBODY who would think to run and hide out here in the Swiss Alps unless they were hiding drug money, but the view that I was staring out at from the balcony door was convincing me.

"Why Switzerland?" I asked, not bothering to then around but knowing that she was listening.

"Why not Switzerland? I mean, it's beautiful here year-round, plus it's not a place that an enemy can just sneak up on. You gotta have money in order to move with the shakers out here, and this is literally the last place a muthafucka would think to come."

I didn't have to turn to look at her to know that she was smiling because she thought that this place was beyond anyone's reach, but that was a miscalculation on her part. It was a deadly mistake, so the question was how to make her pay for it.

"It is beautiful. I'll give you that. How long have you been coming out here?" I asked.

"For years. Viktor used to take important business meetings out here just because it was one stop shopping when it came to privacy and favorable banking laws. I listened and paid attention, and when the time came, I made sure to buy this place as a kind of insurance policy."

"Makes sense. I've seen a lot of the world, but I mostly thought of Switzerland in terms of vacations and rich women," I confessed.

Her laughter made me turn and look at her.

"I guess I fit the type that you had in mind, huh?"

"Not at all, at least not for this environment. You being a mistress in Florida to a powerful man seemed typical to the point that I didn't think to question it, not even when I'd been told that you were 'connected.' You being a ski bunny to some Texas oil man or corrupt politician who spends her summers in Switzerland shopping with the girls didn't fit you at all," I replied, shaking my head as I looked around.

I knew that my glance looked nothing more than curious, but in reality, I was forming the battle plan in my mind so that opportunity could meet preparation. Something inside me felt like my moment was getting closer. I still didn't have the details of the gun battle that Tynesha had gotten into, but it was obvious based on the fact that Marta had moved us halfway around the world that whatever happened involved me. I wouldn't ask any questions about that though because my ignorance would keep her suspicion at bay. I slowly shuffled away from the balcony and made my way back over to her while contemplating my next move because I knew that the approach had to be just right.

"Are you cooking?" I asked, nodding toward the kitchen.

"Is that what you want?" she countered.

Her question confirmed the thought that I'd had earlier about her being attracted to the darkness and dominant force within me, and I quickly analyzed the advantage that came with this knowledge. I stared at her in silence for a few moments, and then, I looked past her to the men seated in the living room watching us.

"I want to take a shower, and I want you in there with me. Make one of them cook."

Without waiting for a response, I turned and headed back in the direction of the bedroom because I knew that she would follow me even if she didn't want to. I went straight to the bathroom once I was back inside the bedroom, and a few seconds later, she joined me.

"Do you want me to bathe you?" she asked seductively.

"The first thing that I want you to do is cut off all of these zip ties because if I didn't kill you a little while ago in the bedroom then that should tell you that I'm not going to. Not to mention the little insurance policy that we share."

She hesitated for a moment, but then, she cut all of them off like I demanded, and then, she stood in front of me like she was waiting on further instructions. I stepped around her and walked into the shower where I turned on the water, allowing it to rain down on me from above. I could hear her moving behind me, but I didn't give my attention to that simply because I knew part of her expected me to. This was undoubtedly part of the sexual dominance and seduction in her mind, and that was the line along which I wanted her to think. Even after I heard and felt her physical presence inside the shower with me, I still ignored her for a few moments and just let the water cascade over me. When she put her hand on my arm, I allowed her to turn me around to face her, but when she tried handing me the soap and washcloth, I just stared at her blankly.

"I want you to wash my back," she said.

"Wash my dick first."

The smile that popped up on her face was rare, but it was genuine, and it reaffirmed the enjoyment that she was getting from all of this. While she busied herself with the soapy rag and my dick, I was looking around the bathroom, and I spotted part of what I needed immediately because her cell phone was on the sink counter. The odds were great that she was controlling the collar around my neck using her phone because it was never out of her sight nor was the phone out of her reach. The way that she was caressing my dick, I knew that she was distracted by the inevitability of another round of angry fucking, and that signaled my moment to turn the tide.

"If you get it hard, you know that you're gonna have to do something about it, right?" I asked, infusing my tone with the proper amount of desire to sell the illusion of sexual tension.

"You know that I know what to do to you. All you gotta do is tell me what you want and how you want it."

"Turn around and face the wall," I demanded.

Her compliance was instantaneous, and she arched her back slightly to entice me. My left hand went straight into her hair while I used my right to guide my dick up inside of her hot pussy. I fed her two long strokes with patience and restraint as I carefully wrapped her hair around the knuckles on my left hand. I was deliberate in my decision not to pull on her hair and instead use nothing but tenderness in my thorough exploration of her body. I was biding my time, allowing her climax to build stronger with each inch of dick I fed her, and the moment that I felt like I had her body calling to me in that uncontrollable way, I switched the game up. My right hand went to her throat, and once there, I applied pressure with increasing force at the same rate of speed as my strokes until I was pounding her pussy and cutting off her air supply almost completely. I knew that she was lost in the moment, chasing that monstrous orgasm, but instead of introducing her to that again, I introduced her to the real monster. Without warning, I slammed her head into the shower wall hard enough to crack the tile while shutting off her air supply completely.

Panic gripped her, and I could feel it radiating all the way down to her pussy that was spasming and clenching wildly. I pulled my dick out of her, but my grip around her throat and hair increased as I slammed her head into the wall again and again until she passed out. There was no turning back now. I quickly carried her out of the shower and laid her on the bathroom floor, but I made sure to leave the water running in case her men were listening. After that, I grabbed her phone and went to work, hacking the collar around my neck first. I made sure to reroute her security protocol and put it under my control so that I could safely remove the collar and put it on her slender neck. When that was done, I sent a message to Destiny through the dark web with my current location, knowing that only she would get the message and not someone aligned with Marta and her bullshit. I knew that my family had enough enemies to make a lot of people want to be Marta's friend if she had the upper hand over one of us, so the paranoia I felt had me thinking outside the box.

Once that was done, I hurriedly put my underwear back on and crept quietly back into the bedroom. The bedroom door was open, and I could hear voices coming from the living room, but it was coming from a distance too great to understand what the conversation was out there. To me, that meant that no one knew what was going on yet, but I knew that my time was definitely short. I made a beeline for the dresser sitting by the bedroom door, and I grabbed the black Taurus 9mm off of it. As quietly as possible, I checked the clip and the chamber, and I felt pressure because I only had eleven shots to work with. There were five hittas in between the living room and the dining room, with twice as many outside, which meant that I had my work cut out for me. As soon as the shooting started, them niggas outside were sure to come running, and that meant that I needed a plan to offset that. The first thing that I did though was a quick search of the room, and once I found the zip ties, I headed back to the bathroom so that I could immobilize Marta. As badly as I wanted to just shoot this bitch or torture her to death, I knew that I could do neither. I bound her hands first, and then, I gagged her. With her effectively out of the way, I mentally shifted into kill mode because shit was about to get all the way real. I left the bathroom and headed back to the living room, flipping the safety off the gun right before I stepped out into the open. A quick survey of the room gave me the location of who would die and in what order death was calling. The guy standing by the balcony, observing the view, was the first person that I shot, hitting him in the back of the head and spraying his brains all over the balcony's sliding glass door in a beautiful arc. This immediately got the attention of the three men watching the soccer game from their seated positions on the white leather couch, but their reaction time was slow, almost like they didn't believe what they were seeing. I swung the gun toward them, already tapping the trigger to deliver two bullets express mail to each man's face and leaving the pristine white leather dripping with bright red blood like a PETA protest. The expression on the man's face who was in the kitchen, cooking, was comical because he had a pan with eggs in it in one hand and a spatula in the other.

"I know this can't be how you saw your life ending, huh?" I asked, chuckling as I shot him right between the eyes.

The overall roar of the gunfire hadn't been as loud as I'd anticipated, and being that no one had gotten a shot off in return, I knew that there was a good possibility that the niggas outside hadn't heard shit. Still, I tucked the pistol I'd used inside my underwear and picked up one of the dead men's AK-47s. I found the nigga closest to my size, stripped the clothes off of him, and quickly got dressed to look the part of a hired hitta for the Zeta Cartel. I made sure to add extra clips of ammo for the AK and anything else helpful.

While I was doing all of this, I was suddenly startled by a radio check that came across the air waves, and I froze for a second.

"Well, are you gonna answer him or nah?" I asked the dead man closest to me.

In all seriousness, the choice I had to make was simple. Either I was going to answer and try to play shit off like it was all good up here or I could invite everyone inside for something that would surely heat them up by the fire. I paused for a second, and then, I responded in rapid Spanish. I told them that the boss was in the shower, and we were watching football until breakfast was ready, while they were out there freezing their nuts off. Naturally, I got cussed out in a good-natured way and told to let them know when breakfast and coffee were ready because the men out there needed it. I agreed and released the breath I'd been holding. My mind was racing, trying to figure out which way to go from here, but so far, all I could see were the tall odds that seemed insurmountable. The longer that I stayed in one spot, the greater the odds of me losing the slim advantage that I'd managed to carve out, but I could see no clear path through the ten-man army outside.

"Unless I just walk through them," I said aloud as a crazy idea started to take shape in my mind.

I quickly went around the room, searching every man's pockets, keeping useful things like cash and phones, but I was looking for something specific. It wasn't until I got to the cook that I found what I was looking for in the form of keys for the Range Rover, and then, I felt my hope growing because now I had access to a getaway vehicle. I was still a long way away from safe, but shit was looking up.

I swiftly hooked a radio and earpiece to my belt and pulled on a baklava to conceal my face as much as possible. With the AK-47 in my grip, I knew that I looked like another worker from a distance, but the odds were good that these niggas knew each other personally at this point, so I definitely couldn't mingle and blend. My only hope was to keep it moving like I had every right to do whatever the fuck I wanted to do. Before I could second guess myself or allow my imagination to create a problem that didn't exist, I headed out the door into the brisk morning air.

As soon as the front door opened, I saw heads turn in my direction, causing me to immediately go on a tirade in Spanish about how the boss wanted me to go into town for fresh cheese and fresh bread. I played my role like my life depended on it, shaking my head and cursing the Swiss who couldn't cook anywhere near as good as my deceased, sainted mother.

I could hear some men laughing, while others agreed and wished to return back home to Mexico as soon as possible. No one had moved to open the tall, steel gate that was literally standing in between me and my freedom though, and that did make me feel a little apprehensive. I kept my cool though as I slid behind the wheel of the SUV and started the engine. The question came through the earpiece about whether or not I wanted someone to ride with me, but I declined quickly and pulled off. When I got to the gate, I had to slow down a little as it was being opened, but my heart was hammering in my chest because, at the same time, I could see a man in the rearview mirror going into the house I'd just left.

The moment that I saw the door open and him walk inside, I knew that my time was up, but I didn't panic. It seemed like an eternity before the gate was open enough for me to push the Range Rover through without losing my side mirrors, and as soon as I hit the gas, I heard screaming followed by shooting.

News of my escape was broadcast loudly, and I heard it in my ear right before the back window of the SUV was shattered into dust by the bullets looking for me. I kept my foot on the gas and my eyes on the winding road in front of me, trying to put big distance between myself and the bullets that undoubtedly had my name on them. I could tell that it hadn't dawned on them that I was still listening to them because they were steadily trying to coordinate my capture over the earpiece and radio, and I was listening intently. At first, I didn't see anyone behind me, even though I could hear how mad and determined they were to get me back. I kept my foot mashed to the floor on top of the gas pedal, but the twists and turns of the road I was navigating made driving like this a certain death wish.

The mountain side was treacherous, with few guardrails at the curves, but there was no other road to run down. The only good thing was that it was a level playing field in terms of them having to drive this same road, but they were doing it using caution. That meant that all I had to do was outrun them, and I had an advantage because of the head start, so I felt good about my odds at the moment. As soon as I heard the word 'helicopter' come through over the earpiece, I felt the advantage evaporate. Experience had taught me that the only thing that outran a helicopter was a radio, and the adrenaline of this knowledge inspired a desperation that I could suddenly taste on my tongue. So, I drove faster. I could hear the roar of an engine, which forced my eyes to the rearview mirror for a second, but it was a second too long. The black ice on the road in front of me was seen too late, the correction that I tried to make to avoid it was done too late, and the result was unavoidable. Suddenly, my view through the windshield became as picturesque as filming a Hollywood sunrise sequence but quickly shifted ,and then, all I could see was the treetops that I was going to hit next.

Chapter 16

(David) (Two Days Later - Florida)

"Is your dog normally this hyper?" Carrie asked.

"No, no, she's just happy to see me because it's been more than a year since I had to give her to my neighbor. A life on the run was no place for Stoney, and I knew that, so I did what I had to do to protect my baby," I replied, continuing to scratch her behind her ears as she jumped up and down on me.

It had been me, Carrie, Rashawna, and Stoney in my condo for the last couple of days while we'd been waiting on Tynesha. Stoney had been running wall to wall since my home girl, Jennifer, brought her home to me. I was just as happy to see my dog as she was to see me because she'd been like one of my children long before I had children, and it had been difficult not to have her with me every day. For a second, everything seemed like it once was, but then reality would come crashing back in whenever I looked at the face of my daughter.

She was beautiful, and she was a perfect blending of me and Ty, but her presence came with complications. The nurse named Crystal that Ty had convinced to protect our daughter had done what was asked of her, and then, she'd taken shit one step too far. By trying to claim our daughter as her own, she'd had the game fucked up. I could understand her doing that to avoid suspicion from the outside world, but trying to stand on that shit with me was where it had gone sideways.

Rashawna was my daughter, but Crystal didn't admit that until she was drawing her last breath.

"David?"

"Huh?" I replied, startled out of my thoughts.

"You didn't hear anything I said, did you?" Carrie asked, tilting her head to the side and looking at me.

"Did you say something else about Stormy?"

"No, I said something about Deante," she replied.

My eyes came up from Stoney's head and immediately locked on Carrie's face as my heart began to beat faster.

"Wh-What about Deante?"

"His nanny said that they'll be here within the hour," she replied calmly.

I could feel myself nodding, but I really couldn't say that I was fully comprehending what this moment meant. When Carrie and I had talked about the son that we'd created together, she'd told me the details of his life thus far, and it was still hard to believe. Deante was two months old, and he lived in the apartment where Carrie and I had conceived him because that was where she'd moved after her and her husband separated. Her pregnancy was the reason that she was separated and pending a divorce because her husband couldn't have more kids, which meant she'd cheated. The rest of her kids had stayed with her ex-husband, and I knew that hurt her tremendously even though it was a mutual decision among the adults. As far as I could tell, her marriage had been over long before her and I started fucking, but we still hadn't discussed what that meant for her now that her and I had a son together.

"You're bringing him here to meet me?" I asked.

"Obviously, but I want him to go to Africa too with his siblings until the smoke clears with all of this. You told me that you were gonna protect all of your kids."

"And I will. That's my word. We gotta tell Ty the truth though because if she doesn't hear it from us then shit could go real REAL bad," I said.

"Shit, you don't know the half of it," she mumbled under her breath.

"What's that mean, Carrie?"

"Nothing, let's just focus on what happens next," she replied.

"Don't do that. Don't shield your thoughts from me like that because we're better than that."

For a moment, she just stared at me, but it was weird because I couldn't read her the way that I normally could, and I didn't like that.

"No more secrets," I insisted.

"Are you sure that's what you want, David?"

"Obviously. I mean, shit, look where we are. You didn't do this by yourself, and you shouldn't have to go through it by yourself. You can trust me and know that I got you," I said genuinely.

She took a deep breath, and that told me how heavy the burden was that she was carrying.

"You wanna tell Ty about our child, and I get your reasons for wanting to do that, but I'm worried about how she's gonna react. I know that she admitted to killing Shaomi, but she never told you how that whole situation went down. It wasn't self-defense or to save your life. It was coldblooded. She made the nurses and doctor stop operating on her, and then she shot her in the head because she refused to let her win again. She refused to let her have another baby with you and therefore create another life and future with you. This is what she did to her own cousin, her family, so what the fuck do you think she's gonna do with me?"

Her question was entirely valid, and there was no quick response that popped into my mind. I didn't second guess Carrie's story in the slightest when it came to how Shaomi died because I could still remember the look in Ty's eyes when I'd found her down in the glades with her sister and two hostages. Umar letting Tynesha and Tesha torture Viktor's family had infected them with a lust for blood, and there were few things that could stand in the way of quenching that hunger. I wasn't afraid of my wife, and I didn't think that Carrie was either, but we were both aware of how ugly this shit could get.

"What other option do you see?" I asked, looking Carrie in the eyes.

"I feel like asking you to deny your son or not be a part of his life makes me no better than Tesha, so we've gotta figure out a different way. I honestly just don't know what that is."

"What if we told her that we didn't start fucking around until after shit went sideways with her and Roland?" I asked.

"She's not gonna care when we started fucking, David. She's only gonna care that yet another bitch has a baby with you."

There was no way for me to argue with this logic, just like there were no easy solutions, and we were running out of time to plan.

"Okay, well, we can still send Deante to Africa with the rest of the kids by simply explaining that he's your son. Ty won't question that because she knows that you've been in this with us from the beginning of the bullshit," I said.

"She might question why I'm only sending this particular child and not my other kids."

"You're right, she could, but I'm thinking that she'll be too preoccupied with Rashawna to really focus on the details, and we have to keep her thoughts on anything except for you and I," I replied.

Carrie nodded as she stood up and crossed the room to me while holding my daughter in her arms.

"I guess we should get this out of the way before she gets here," Carrie said, grabbing me by a fistful of my shirt to pull me toward her.

She kissed me like it was our first time and she was excited, combined with it being a last kiss that she wanted to remember. By the time she took a step back, she'd effectively turned my mind to mush, and it stayed like that until Stoney started barking right before she bolted for the door.

"Your dog is crazy," Carrie said, laughing.

"No, she's smart. Someone is at the door, and being that Stoney is excited, I'd guess that it's Tynesha."

"Oh. Well, go open the door," she said, taking another step back.

"No need for that."

The inquisitive look that she gave me disappeared when she heard the front door open and Stoney losing her damn mind like when she saw me.

"There's my girl! Hi, Stoney! Did you miss me?" Ty asked, giggling.

I could feel the smile tugging at my lips despite the fear that I saw in Carrie's eyes.

"It's okay, just chill," I said, gently taking Rashawna from her and turning toward the sound of Ty coming up the hallway.

As soon as Ty hit the corner, her eyes dropped to our beautiful baby girl in my arms, and the overwhelming emotions came shining through in the tears that filled her eyes.

"This is your daughter, Rashawna," I said, holding her out to Ty.

Her footsteps faltered for a second, but she recovered quickly and pulled Rashawna toward her. She couldn't say anything, so she just cried silently while hugging her close. I nodded toward Carrie, indicating that we should give Ty some privacy, and we both quietly stepped away. I was wanting to head for the kitchen, but Carrie took me by the hand and led me toward the front door and outside into the hallway.

"Where are we going?" I asked.

Her response was to pass me her phone where I saw a text message that had popped up a minute ago from someone saying that they were out front. My stomach dropped in anticipation, but I kept my cool and walked with Carrie outside.

"Hey, La La, thanks for bringing him," Carrie said.

"No problem. You know that I'd do anything for my godson... Plus I wanted to get a look at the man who you went half on a baby with."

"Omg, La La, shut up and don't start," Carrie said.

"Okay, okay, but you didn't lie. I would've fucked him too."

"Are we really gonna talk about me like I'm not standing right here?" I asked, chuckling.

"Yes, yes, we are," La La replied.

Carrie just shook her head as she opened the rear door and got Deante out of the car seat before passing him straight to me. He was sleeping peacefully, looking so angelic that I felt myself choking up, and I had to fight to remain calm because I didn't want to scare him.

"He's so tiny," I said.

"Yeah, he's only six and a half pounds, but the boy eats like he's fifteen years old already," Carrie replied, chuckling as she passed me the diaper bag.

I could see my features on his face, but it wasn't so blatant that I thought Ty would just look at him and know.

"What color are his eyes?" I asked.

"You'll see when he wakes up. In the meantime, we need to decide how to play this," Carrie replied.

"Just trust me. I'll keep you both safe."

"If I had a penny for every time I heard that shit then..."

"Bye, La La. Thanks for coming. Get home safe," Carrie said, interrupting her friend's tirade while pushing her toward the car door.

My focus remained on Deante and the instant connection that I could feel with him already. Deep down, I knew that this was my son, and that knowledge made me feel more blessed than I could put into words. As I moved toward the building, I felt Carrie fall into step with me, but she didn't speak despite the anxiety rolling off of her in waves.

"It's gonna be fine," I said.

"I hope you're right, but I'm telling you, David, if I even THINK that she means to harm me or my son, I'mma smoke her muthafuckin ass. No hesitation, no apologies."

"It won't get to that," I said, looking over at her.

"I know that you truly wanna believe that, but I know that you're not blind or naïve, which means that you see how much Tynesha and Tesha have both changed. When Ty finds out about our son, this shit can definitely go left."

When I looked back down at my son, I knew that I couldn't let anything happen to him or Carrie, which meant that I needed to do something different than I had before at times like this. I needed to take control.

"Okay, listen. Just let me do all the talking when we get back inside," I stated.

"Oh, God, I don't like the sound of this, David. What the fuck are you gonna say?"

"I'm gonna tell her a believable lie and say that we got high and drunk one night. The end," I replied.

"And you really think that she's gonna go for that?! I'm telling you that it ain't gonna matter how accidental me getting pregnant was. All that she will care about is the fact that you and I fucked."

"Ordinarily you'd probably be right, but that problem ain't a issue that she has time to dwell on right now. Did you see her with Rashawna? Just trust me," I said, leading the way back inside.

We rode in silence up to my condo, and when we got to the door, I handed Deante back to her.

"Stay behind me and shield Deante no matter what," I instructed.

She nodded, and we both took deep breaths before entering my condo. I could hear Ty talking to Rashawna in a voice that had her cooing in agreement, and that warmed my heart. I found them sitting in the middle of the living room, with Stoney standing guard, and it made me laugh out loud while thinking about us playing on the floor back in the day.

"The more things change, the more they stay the same," I said.

Ty's eyes flickered up at me, and I saw a contentment within her that had been missing. It made me happy because this was a moment I had given her, and I knew that she would cherish it.

"She's amazing, David. Come here," Ty beckoned, motioning for me to get on the floor with her and Rashawna.

I laid right down on the other side of my baby girl, and she immediately began to look back and forth between me and Ty.

"You think that she knows who we are yet?" I asked.

"I don't know, but babies are smart, and their instincts are uncanny. I can't say for sure, but there's something about the way that her eyes light up when she looks at me that makes me feel like her soul recognizes me. I know it sounds crazy but..."

"It doesn't sound crazy, sweetheart," I said, reaching out and taking a hold of Ty's hand.

She smiled at me with tears in her eyes, but then, the impatient buzzing of her phone interrupted the moment. As she pulled her phone out, I turned my attention to Carrie who'd been standing a few feet away, quietly rocking Deante. The nervousness that she felt was still engrained in every line of her beautiful face, but when I gave her a reassuring wink, she managed to give me a half smile.

"We might've just got lucky," Ty said with obvious excitement.

"How?" I asked quickly.

"I just got word that Marta took her show on the road and moved Rashon and Royal after that shit went sideways between me and Tesha in Mexico City. The bug that I planted in her living room picked up on her men talking, and they revealed that she's in Geneva, Switzerland," Ty said, smiling broadly.

"Who the fuck hides in Switzerland?" I asked.

"Someone with money to blend in," Carrie said.

"Exactly, and we can play that role with her because we're African royalty," Ty replied, obviously warming up to the idea.

"Okay, so what's the plan?" I asked.

"We slip into Switzerland because she's not expecting it, and it would be impossible for her to be inconspicuous with a whole team of goons, so I'm betting that she's running on a skeleton crew compared to Mexico City," Ty replied.

I thought about what she said, and it sounded logical and plausible, but I needed more facts.

"Give me some time to hack into satellite footage and any cameras out there. I think that the easiest approach will be to have Interpol hit her with a red notice, which will basically cause her to be detained at the request of Ghana," I said.

"Will Ghana actually issue that request?" Carrie asked.

"Of course we will. I am the king, and this woman is wanted for war crimes," I replied, pulling my own phone out and scrolling through the contacts.

All it would take was a call from General Udoku.

"Uh, Carrie, where did that baby come from?" Ty asked.

I could feel Carrie stop breathing, but she kept her cool and managed to laugh the question off.

"My home girl dropped him off a little while ago. It's been too long since I saw him, so I figured that I could spend some time with him since we had to come back down south to track that nurse."

"I didn't realize that you'd had a baby recently or that you were even pregnant, bitch! Congratulations," Ty said.

My eyes still stayed glued to my phone, but I knew Ty's tone, and there were definitely more questions than answers at this point. Which meant more questions were coming.

"Carrie, I want you to take the kids to Ghana, and Ty, I want you to come with me to Switzerland so that we can get out son," I said.

"I can do that." Carrie readily agreed.

"Soooo, are we *not* gonna talk about your son being my husband's baby?" Ty asked.

Chapter 17

(Tynesha)

The silence that followed my comment was louder than the chorus of the devil's angels that had been singing after I'd killed Shaomi. My memory of the hatred that I'd felt in that moment was so vivid that I could feel myself getting hot now, but I gave myself a little mental shake to balance me back out.

"Cat got both of your tongues?" I asked.

"Ty, listen, I..."

"On second thought, shut up, David. I wanna hear what Carrie has to say," I said, locking eyes with one of my oldest and dearest friends.

"You wanna hear what I have to say? What can I say for real, Ty? What the fuck do you want me to say?" she asked, showing signs of exasperation with the topic of conversation already.

"How bout you telling me the truth and let's see how that works out for you?" I replied, feeling my anger stirring awake despite the calmness that my daughter provided.

"The truth, huh? Well, you know, everybody wants the truth when that shit is watered down and sweetened, but the shit that you're asking for is more lethal than fentanyl and heroin cut with battery acid," she warned.

"Ohhh, sounds scary," I replied mockingly.

"Ty, just let it go and let's focus back on the mission because we still have a son out there missing," David said.

"I know what the mission is, David, just like I knew that your hoe ass couldn't resist the urge to step in and try to save this bitch," I said, looking back and forth between him and Carrie with disgust.

"You want the truth, bitch? First, let me start by saying that you're *welcome*! While your silly ass was doing everything that you could to break and destroy this man, I was holding him up and making sure that he remembered why he wears a crown. Nah, I didn't do it by taking the dick every chance that I got or trying to manipulate my way inside the family. I just kept it as real with him as possible. I didn't allow him to lose himself when you flipped sides and started literally fucking the opps. I stood in the trenches with him, ten toes down like a real bitch, and I STILL never tried to take your spot when so many other hoes were fighting for the crown! I ain't trying to sit here and act like I'm not in the wrong for fucking David because I am, but at least my motives behind it were clear. I only ever wanted to see him win," she stated.

"Even if that fight was with me, you still wanted to see him win? You supposed to be MY bitch, my muthafuckin home girl from back in the day, and that means that you don't get to pick a side unless it's mine. How do you not get that?" I asked heatedly.

"Tynesha, you done lost your goddamn mind for real. I ain't no 'yes man' or no flunky ass bitch. I'm my own woman, and you knew that a long time ago. I don't know why you acting like this is brand new now. I been the type to stand on bidness, and this ain't no different. How you wanna carry it is up to you though," she replied, handing her son to David without taking her eyes off of mine.

Part of me wanted to drag this bitch on the spot, but the other part of me was kind of impressed with the way that she was handling the situation. She was definitely wrong, and so was he, but I couldn't act like I wasn't wrong either. So, either we all killed each other or we learned to let that shit live so that our kids actually had someone around to raise them. Carrie wasn't my opp because she wasn't trying to take my spot or steal my crown. She was just part of this dysfunctional family now, and that meant giving her the same amount of forgiveness that I wanted. When I looked down at my daughter, I could see her daddy in her features, just like I could when it came to the little boy in David's arms. All of our kids were beautiful and made from love in some form, which meant that they were a blessing to all of us, even though we probably didn't deserve it.

"He's gorgeous," I said, nodding toward their son.

"And so is she," Carrie replied, stepping forward and taking one of my hands in hers.

"What's his name?" I asked.

"Deante Tyrese Bishop," Carrie replied.

I could tell by the surprised look on David's face that he'd never heard his son's whole name before, but he immediately understood the significance.

"Y-You added part of my name into his," I said, looking at her with disbelief.

"Of course I did, bitch. You're his godmother after all."

I could feel the prick of tears stinging the backs of my eyelids, but this was most definitely not the time for water works or mushy shit.

"I hate you for making me cry," I said, swiping at the rogue tear sliding down my face as I laughed.

Unexpectedly, she pulled me into a quick hug and whispered that she loved me, and just like that, everything was okay again. David's phone ringing startled us all, which made him laugh and caused little Deante to stir awake.

"What's up, Udoku?" David said, answering his phone.

In that moment, I was smacked in the face by the ugly reality that I'd been travelling with, but I could already tell that the general was unintentionally delivering the bad news. The moment that David's eyes hardened into tiny black marbles, I knew that he was on demon time, and I quickly pulled Carrie to me so that she would understand what happened.

"Oh, shit," she mumbled, looking at me in both sympathy and understanding of how volatile David would be with news like this on his shoulders.

"We will have a ceremony for him once we have completed the mission of gathering all of my children together, like he wanted. For now, I need that red notice issued and enforced by the time we get to Switzerland. Call me with updates," he said, disconnecting the call.

"David, I was coming to tell you in person because..."

"I know, and I get it. The general said that you handled yourself like a true queen, and I want you to know that I appreciate that," he said calmly.

Carrie and I exchanged a look, which told me that I wasn't just hearing and seeing things that weren't there. This nigga has shut down right in front of us, and we understood the danger in that.

"David, it's okay to feel sad or be fucked up about losing you uncle," Carrie said softly.

"I know that, but I'm fine. Let's just get to what happens next," he replied.

I wasn't trying to piss him off, and something told me to just let it go for now.

"What do you think happens next?" I asked, trying to remain diplomatic and compromising.

"Well... with Marta in Switzerland, I'd say that the Zeta Cartel is more vulnerable than they've ever been, and they wouldn't be expecting an attack. I'll use our people in Sinaloa for that because that will be the token of peace needed to prevent us from an all-out war with the Mexican Mafia. The Swiss authorities will detain Marta, along with rescuing Rashon, which means that we need to show up and get him."

"How are you gonna do that without your name appearing on any official documentation as it relates to him?" Carrie asked.

"Simple. His mom is going to get him, and she'll do all the talking."

David's comment caused me and Carrie to look at each other, but neither of us understood where this was going.

"Care to explain?" I asked.

"After sitting down with Tesha in Texas, I finally realized how determined she is to be a part or the Walker family and destroy everyone else who isn't a part or that clan. So, I've decided to see how she handles becoming who she wants to be when she can't prove who she is. There will be no record of twins being born, no record of you two ever existing at the same time. In fact, there's a pretty thick file that speaks about 'Tynesha Bishop's' mental health,' specifically about her split personality disorder that the judge reviewing her for competency to stand trial for capital murder is currently in possession of. So, Tesha will stay locked up because she never really existed, only Tynesha does. And while she's doing that, you'll be showing up with a diplomatic passport saying that you're Tynesha Bishop, queen of Ghana and Rashon's mother/legal guardian. This will allow him to be turned over to you, and there's no one to argue against either of our legal rights to our son. Once that's done, and we have all of the kids, then we become invisible until it's time to attack," he replied.

"Attack? Attack who? David?" I asked.

"We will attack and destroy those who tried to do the same to us. Zoe Pound, the cartels, the fucking U.S. government... And we can't forget the Walker family too. They must die painfully, slowly, and very, *very* publicly..."

Chapter 18

(FatherGod) (Six Months Later)

"The Honorable Judge Jason Nathaniel, it's nice to finally meet you. I've heard a lot about you. My name is Jonathan Walker, but those that know me call me FATHERGOD. Have you heard of me?" I asked, watching him closely.

He couldn't speak or move because he was bound and gagged to the chair in the middle of his living room, but the terror that clouded his eyes told me that he absolutely knew who I was.

"I'm glad that my reputation has preceded me because that means that I can dispense with the threats and torture. Now, obviously, you weren't expecting me because I've been 'legally' dead for a number of years now, but your actions have directly affected my extended, private vacation, and I wanted to speak with you about that. Do you know what I'm talking about?" I asked calmly.

He uttered not a sound, and the fear continued to grow with the speed of a sunrise chasing away nighttime shadows.

"I'm here about one of my daughters, a woman that you refer to as Tynesha Bishop. Now, you and I both know that the woman that you tried and convicted for capital murder isn't actually Tynesha Bishop, but for whatever reason, you let the circus into your courtroom, and now, I'm forced to intervene. Which brings me to my point, Your Honor. You will declare Tynesha Bishop competent to stand trial at her appeal, and you will ensure that she walks out of court with a clean record. Do you understand?" I asked.

I still got no movement, not even a blink of the eyes to emphasize his distress, and that was very trying for my patience. I pulled out my pretty, black Glock. 34 with the switch on it that was equipped with the custom fifty-round transparent drum that lit up with flames as the bullets spun and cycled into the chamber. To the judge's left sat his wife, Kelly, and to his right sat his sister, Brenda.

"I know where your kids are too, Judge Nathaniel, so the question is how many funerals do you wanna attend this weekend?"

Before he answered, I shot his wife and sister in the face, which finally made him blink. And then, his bitch ass passed out...

2 be continued...

Lock Down Publications and Ca$h Presents
Assisted Publishing Packages

BASIC PACKAGE	UPGRADED PACKAGE
$499	$800
Editing	Typing
Cover Design	Editing
Formatting	Cover Design
	Formatting
ADVANCE PACKAGE	**LDP SUPREME PACKAGE**
$1,200	$1,500
Typing	Typing
Editing	Editing
Cover Design	Cover Design
Formatting	Formatting
Copyright registration	Copyright registration
Proofreading	Proofreading
Upload book to Amazon	Set up Amazon account
	Upload book to Amazon
	Advertise on LDP, Amazon and
	Facebook Page

***Other services available upon request.
Additional charges may apply

Lock Down Publications
P.O. Box 944
Stockbridge, GA 30281-9998
Phone: 470 303-9761

Submission Guideline

Submit the first three chapters of your completed manuscript to ldpsubmissions@gmail.com. In the subject line add **Your Book's Title**. The manuscript must be in a Word Doc file and sent as an attachment. Document should be in Times New Roman, double spaced, and in size 12 font. Also, provide your synopsis and full contact information. If sending multiple submissions, they must each be in a separate email.

Have a story but no way to send it electronically? You can still submit to LDP/Ca$h Presents. Send in the first three chapters, written or typed, of your completed manuscript to:

LDP: Submissions Dept
P.O. Box 944
Stockbridge, GA 30281-9998

DO NOT send original manuscript. Must be a duplicate.
Provide your synopsis and a cover letter containing your full contact information.

Thanks for considering LDP and Ca$h Presents.

NEW RELEASES

BLOODLINE OF A SAVAGE 1&2
THESE VICIOUS STREETS
RELENTLESS GOON
RELENTLESS GOON 2
BY PRINCE A. TAUHID

THE BUTTERFLY MAFIA 1-3
BY FUMIYA PAYNE

A THUG'S STREET PRINCESS 1&2
BY MEESHA

CITY OF SMOKE 2
BY MOLOTTI

STEPPERS 1,2&3
BY KING RIO

THE LANE 1&2
BY KEN-KEN SPENCE

THUG OF SPADES 1&2
LOVE IN THE TRENCHES 2
BY COREY ROBINSON

TIL DEATH 3
BY ARYANNA

THE BIRTH OF A GANGSTER 4
BY DELMONT PLAYER

PRODUCT OF THE STREETS 1&2
BY DEMOND "MONEY" ANDERSON

NO TIME FOR ERROR
BY KEESE

MONEY HUNGRY DEMONS
BY TRANAY ADAMS

Coming Soon from Lock Down Publications/Ca$h Presents

IF YOU CROSS ME ONCE 6
ANGEL V
By Anthony Fields

IMMA DIE BOUT MINE 4&5
By Aryanna

A THUGS STREET PRINCESS 3
By Meesha

PRODUCT OF THE STREETS 3
By Demond Money Anderson

CORNER BOYS
By Corey Robinson

SON OF A DOPE FIEND 4
By Renta

THE MURDER QUEENS 6&7
By Michael Gallon

CITY OF SMOKE 3
By Molotti

BETRAYAL OF A G
By Ray Vinci

CONFESSIONS OF A DOPE BOY
By Nicholas Lock

THA TAKEOVER
By Keith Chandler

Available Now

RESTRAINING ORDER 1 & 2
By **CA$H & Coffee**

LOVE KNOWS NO BOUNDARIES 1-3
By **Coffee**

RAISED AS A GOON I, II, III & IV
BRED BY THE SLUMS I, II, III
BLAST FOR ME I & II
ROTTEN TO THE CORE I II III
A BRONX TALE I, II, III
DUFFLE BAG CARTEL I II III IV V VI
HEARTLESS GOON I II III IV V
A SAVAGE DOPEBOY I II
DRUG LORDS I II III
CUTTHROAT MAFIA I II
KING OF THE TRENCHES
By **Ghost**

LAY IT DOWN I & II
LAST OF A DYING BREED I II
BLOOD STAINS OF A SHOTTA I & II III
By **Jamaica**

LOYAL TO THE GAME I II III
LIFE OF SIN I, II III
By **TJ & Jelissa**

IF LOVING HIM IS WRONG…I & II
LOVE ME EVEN WHEN IT HURTS I II III
By **Jelissa**

BLOODY COMMAS I & II
SKI MASK CARTEL I, II & III
KING OF NEW YORK I II, III IV V
RISE TO POWER I II III
COKE KINGS I II III IV V
BORN HEARTLESS I II III IV
KING OF THE TRAP I II
By **T.J. Edwards**

WHEN THE STREETS CLAP BACK I & II III
THE HEART OF A SAVAGE I II III IV
MONEY MAFIA I II
LOYAL TO THE SOIL I II III
By **Jibril Williams**

A DISTINGUISHED THUG STOLE MY HEART I II &
III
LOVE SHOULDN'T HURT I II III IV
RENEGADE BOYS 1-4
PAID IN KARMA 1-3
SAVAGE STORMS 1-3
AN UNFORESEEN LOVE 1-3
BABY, I'M WINTERTIME COLD 1-3
A THUG'S STREET PRINCESS 1&2
By **Meesha**

A GANGSTER'S CODE 1-3
A GANGSTER'S SYN 1-3
THE SAVAGE LIFE 1-3
CHAINED TO THE STREETS 1-3
BLOOD ON THE MONEY 1-3
A GANGSTA'S PAIN 1-3
BEAUTIFUL LIES AND UGLY TRUTHS
CHURCH IN THESE STREETS
By **J-Blunt**

PUSH IT TO THE LIMIT
By **Bre' Hayes**

BLOOD OF A BOSS 1-5
SHADOWS OF THE GAME
TRAP BASTARD
By **Askari**

THE STREETS BLEED MURDER 1-3
THE HEART OF A GANGSTA 1-3
By **Jerry Jackson**

CUM FOR ME 1-8
An LDP Erotica Collaboration

BRIDE OF A HUSTLA 1-3
THE FETTI GIRLS 1-3
CORRUPTED BY A GANGSTA 1-4
BLINDED BY HIS LOVE
THE PRICE YOU PAY FOR LOVE 1-3
DOPE GIRL MAGIC 1-3
By **Destiny Skai**

WHEN A GOOD GIRL GOES BAD
By **Adrienne**

A KINGPIN'S AMBITION
A KINGPIN'S AMBITION II
I MURDER FOR THE DOUGH
By **Ambitious**

THE COST OF LOYALTY 1-3
By **Kweli**

A GANGSTER'S REVENGE 1-4
THE BOSS MAN'S DAUGHTERS 1-5
A SAVAGE LOVE 1&2
BAE BELONGS TO ME 1&2
A HUSTLER'S DECEIT 1-3
WHAT BAD BITCHES DO 1-3
SOUL OF A MONSTER 1-3
KILL ZONE
A DOPE BOY'S QUEEN 1-3
TIL DEATH 1-3
IMMA DIE BOUT MINE 1-3
By **Aryanna**

TRUE SAVAGE 1-7
DOPE BOY MAGIC 1-3
MIDNIGHT CARTEL 1-3
CITY OF KINGZ 1&2
NIGHTMARE ON SILENT AVE
THE PLUG OF LIL MEXICO 1&2
CLASSIC CITY
By **Chris Green**

A DOPEBOY'S PRAYER
By **Eddie "Wolf" Lee**

THE KING CARTEL 1-3
By **Frank Gresham**

THESE NIGGAS AIN'T LOYAL 1-3
By **Nikki Tee**

GANGSTA SHYT 1-3
By **CATO**

IMMA DIE BOUT MINE 5 | ARYANNA

THE ULTIMATE BETRAYAL
By **Phoenix**

BOSS'N UP 1-3
By **Royal Nicole**

I LOVE YOU TO DEATH
By **Destiny J**

I RIDE FOR MY HITTA
I STILL RIDE FOR MY HITTA
By **Misty Holt**

LOVE & CHASIN' PAPER
By **Qay Crockett**

TO DIE IN VAIN
SINS OF A HUSTLA
By **ASAD**

BROOKLYN HUSTLAZ
By **Boogsy Morina**

BROOKLYN ON LOCK 1 & 2
By **Sonovia**

GANGSTA CITY
By **Teddy Duke**

A DRUG KING AND HIS DIAMOND 1-3
A DOPEMAN'S RICHES
HER MAN, MINE'S TOO 1&2
CASH MONEY HO'S
THE WIFEY I USED TO BE 1&2
PRETTY GIRLS DO NASTY THINGS
By **Nicole Goosby**

LIPSTICK KILLAH 1-3
CRIME OF PASSION 1-3
FRIEND OR FOE 1-3
By **Mimi**

TRAPHOUSE KING 1-3
KINGPIN KILLAZ 1-3
STREET KINGS 1&2
PAID IN BLOOD 1&2
CARTEL KILLAZ 1-3
DOPE GODS 1&2
By **Hood Rich**

STEADY MOBBN' 1-3
THE STREETS STAINED MY SOUL 1-3
By **Marcellus Allen**

WHO SHOT YA 1-3
SON OF A DOPE FIEND 1-3
HEAVEN GOT A GHETTO 1&2
SKI MASK MONEY 1&2
By **Renta**

GORILLAZ IN THE BAY 1-4
TEARS OF A GANGSTA 1/&2
3X KRAZY 1&2
STRAIGHT BEAST MODE 1&2
By **DE'KARI**

TRIGGADALE 1-3
MURDA WAS THE CASE 1-3
By **Elijah R. Freeman**

THE STREETS ARE CALLING
By **Duquie Wilson**

SLAUGHTER GANG 1-3
RUTHLESS HEART 1-3
By **Willie Slaughter**

GOD BLESS THE TRAPPERS 1-3
THESE SCANDALOUS STREETS 1-3
FEAR MY GANGSTA 1-5
THESE STREETS DON'T LOVE NOBODY 1-2
BURY ME A G 1-5
A GANGSTA'S EMPIRE 1-4
THE DOPEMAN'S BODYGAURD 1&2
THE REALEST KILLAZ 1-3
THE LAST OF THE OGS 1-3
By **Tranay Adams**

MARRIED TO A BOSS 1-3
By **Destiny Skai & Chris Green**

KINGZ OF THE GAME 1-7
CRIME BOSS 1-3
By **Playa Ray**

FUK SHYT
By **Blakk Diamond**

DON'T F#CK WITH MY HEART 1&2
By **Linnea**

ADDICTED TO THE DRAMA 1-3
IN THE ARM OF HIS BOSS
By **Jamila**

LOYALTY AIN'T PROMISED 1&2
By **Keith Williams**

YAYO 1-4
A SHOOTER'S AMBITION 1&2
BRED IN THE GAME
By **S. Allen**

TRAP GOD 1-3
RICH $AVAGE 1-3
MONEY IN THE GRAVE 1-3
CARTEL MONEY
By **Martell Troublesome Bolden**

FOREVER GANGSTA 1&2
GLOCKS ON SATIN SHEETS 1&2
By **Adrian Dulan**

TOE TAGZ 1-4
LEVELS TO THIS SHYT 1&2
IT'S JUST ME AND YOU
By **Ah'Million**

KINGPIN DREAMS 1-3
RAN OFF ON DA PLUG
By **Paper Boi Rari**

CONFESSIONS OF A GANGSTA 1-4
CONFESSIONS OF A JACKBOY 1-3
CONFESSIONS OF A HITMAN
By **Nicholas Lock**

I'M NOTHING WITHOUT HIS LOVE
SINS OF A THUG
TO THE THUG I LOVED BEFORE
A GANGSTA SAVED XMAS
IN A HUSTLER I TRUST
By **Monet Dragun**

QUIET MONEY 1-3
THUG LIFE 1-3
EXTENDED CLIP 1&2
A GANGSTA'S PARADISE
By **Trai'Quan**

CAUGHT UP IN THE LIFE 1-3
THE STREETS NEVER LET GO 1-3
By **Robert Baptiste**

NEW TO THE GAME 1-3
MONEY, MURDER & MEMORIES 1-3
By **Malik D. Rice**

CREAM 2-3
THE STREETS WILL TALK
By **Yolanda Moore**

LIFE OF A SAVAGE 1-4
A GANGSTA'S QUR'AN 1-4
MURDA SEASON 1-3
GANGLAND CARTEL 1-3
CHI'RAQ GANGSTAS 1-4
KILLERS ON ELM STREET 1-3
JACK BOYZ N DA BRONX 1-3
A DOPEBOY'S DREAM 1-3
JACK BOYS VS DOPE BOYS 1-3
COKE GIRLZ
COKE BOYS
SOSA GANG 1&2
BRONX SAVAGES
BODYMORE KINGPINS
BLOOD OF A GOON
By **Romell Tukes**

THE STREETS MADE ME 1-3
By **Larry D. Wright**

CONCRETE KILLA 1-3
VICIOUS LOYALTY 1-3
By **Kingpen**

THE ULTIMATE SACRIFICE 1-6
KHADIFI
IF YOU CROSS ME ONCE 1-3
ANGEL 1-4
IN THE BLINK OF AN EYE
By **Anthony Fields**

THE LIFE OF A HOOD STAR
By **Ca$h & Rashia Wilson**

THE STREETS WILL NEVER CLOSE 1-3
By **K'ajji**

NIGHTMARES OF A HUSTLA 1-3
By **King Dream**

HARD AND RUTHLESS 1&2
MOB TOWN 251
THE BILLIONAIRE BENTLEYS 1-3
REAL G'S MOVE IN SILENCE
By **Von Diesel**

GHOST MOB
By **Stilloan Robinson**

MOB TIES 1-6
SOUL OF A HUSTLER, HEART OF A KILLER 1-3
GORILLAZ IN THE TRENCHES
By **SayNoMore**

BODYMORE MURDERLAND 1-3
THE BIRTH OF A GANGSTER 1-4
By **Delmont Player**

FOR THE LOVE OF A BOSS 1&2
By **C. D. Blue**

KILLA KOUNTY 1-5
By **Khufu**

MOBBED UP 1-4
THE BRICK MAN 1-5
THE COCAINE PRINCESS 1-10
STEPPERS 1-3
SUPER GREMLIN 1-4
By **King Rio**

MONEY GAME 1&2
By **Smoove Dolla**

A GANGSTA'S KARMA 1-4
By **FLAME**

KING OF THE TRENCHES 1-3
By **GHOST & TRANAY ADAMS**

QUEEN OF THE ZOO 1&2
By **Black Migo**

GRIMEY WAYS 1-3
By **Ray Vinci**

XMAS WITH AN ATL SHOOTER
By **Ca$h & Destiny Skai**

IMMA DIE BOUT MINE 5 | ARYANNA

KING KILLA 1&2
By **Vincent "Vitto" Holloway**

BETRAYAL OF A THUG 1&2
By **Fre$h**

THE MURDER QUEENS 1-5
By **Michael Gallon**

FOR THE LOVE OF BLOOD 1-4
By **Jamel Mitchell**

HOOD CONSIGLIERE 1&2
NO TIME FOR ERROR
By **Keese**

PROTÉGÉ OF A LEGEND 1&2
LOVE IN THE TRENCHES 1&2
By **Corey Robinson**

BORN IN THE GRAVE 1-3
CRIME PAYS
By **Self Made Tay**

MOAN IN MY MOUTH
By **XTASY**

TORN BETWEEN A GANGSTER AND A GENTLEMAN
By **J-BLUNT & Miss Kim**

LOYALTY IS EVERYTHING 1-3
CITY OF SMOKE 1&2
By **Molotti**

HERE TODAY GONE TOMORROW 1&2
By **Fly Rock**

WOMEN LIE MEN LIE 1-4
FIFTY SHADES OF SNOW 1-3
STACK BEFORE YOU SPLURGE
GIRLS FALL LIKE DOMINOES
NAÏVE TO THE STREETS
By **ROY MILLIGAN**

PILLOW PRINCESS
By **S. Hawkins**

THE BUTTERFLY MAFIA 1-3
SALUTE MY SAVAGERY 1&2
By **Fumiya Payne**

THE LANE 1&2
By Ken-Ken Spence

THE PUSSY TRAP 1-5
By **Nene Capri**

DIRTY DNA
By **Blaque**

SANCTIFIED AND HORNY
by **XTASY**